The Ties That Bind

Red Phoenix

Copyright © 2021 Red Phoenix
Print Edition
www.redphoenixauthor.com

The Ties That Bind:
Brie's Submission Book 22

Cover by Shanoff Designs
Formatted by BB Books
Phoenix symbol by Nicole Delfs

Dedication

I dedicate The Ties That Bind to my muses!

They took me on an incredible journey I wasn't expecting. I thought I knew where we were headed, but then the story took beautiful twists and turns that completely awed me. However, it was the tender moments in this book that took my breath away and melted my heart.

After we all survived the unexpected death in Her Sweet Surrender, we needed a book full of hope, inspiration and love.

The muses knew this and took us along for the ride!

My muses were not only tender, but sexy as heck in this book.

For me, the best part is near the end. My friends, this is something we have waited a long time for and it is spectacular and glorious.

Heck to the yeah!

Of course, I must thank you for your unwavering support and patience, my dear fans.

Big hugs to my editor Kh Koehler and my wonderful betas, Brenda, Becki, Marilyn, and Kathy.

Extra huge hug to Pippa Jayne who agreed to help me release the audiobook at the same time as the book. You and I have created memories through this endeavor, my courageous friend.

Much love to MrRed, who is forever my knight in shining armor.

SIGN UP FOR MY NEWSLETTER
HERE FOR THE LATEST RED
PHOENIX UPDATES

FOLLOW ME ON INSTAGRAM
INSTAGRAM.COM/REDPHOENIXAUTHOR

SALES, GIVEAWAYS, NEW
RELEASES, PREORDER LINKS, AND
MORE!
SIGN UP HERE
REDPHOENIXAUTHOR.COM/NEWSLETTER-
SIGNUP

CONTENTS

Ambush

Brie was grabbing a quick snack before heading upstairs to work on her next film when she heard the screeching of multiple vehicles braking abruptly, and car doors slamming, just outside their house. Taking a quick peek through the window, she let out a frightened gasp when she saw four black utility vehicles parked outside and an army of men dressed in black suits walking up to the door.

Grabbing Hope, Brie rushed to Sir's office to tell him what was happening.

Without a moment's hesitation, he pushed Brie toward the back door. "Go to Durov's while I find out what these men want."

"Don't face them alone," she cried. "Come with me."

Glancing at Hope squirming in her arms, he commanded, "I don't know their intentions and it will give you time to escape."

Brie knew Sir would give his life to protect them and whimpered when he shut the door behind her. Racing to

Rytsar's with her daughter clutched against her chest, Brie banged on his door, hoping against hope he hadn't left for Russia yet.

While she waited in agony for someone to answer, Brie kept glancing back at their house, praying for Sir's safety.

Rytsar opened the door dressed in a robe that was open but cinched at the waist, showing off his muscular chest. He smirked when he saw her. "Have you come to play before I go, *radost moya*?"

Brie shook her head and rushed inside.

His expression instantly changed as he grabbed Hope from her. "What's wrong?"

Brie could barely speak as she panted, "There are men…lots of them…"

Rytsar frowned. "Where?"

"At the house. Sir insisted on staying behind."

Rytsar growled, calling out to Maxim. "Mobilize my men, now!"

Guiding Brie to Hope's room, he stated, "Stay here and remain quiet until I command otherwise."

Before he shut the door, Rytsar whistled for Little Sparrow. "Watch over them, *Vorobyshek*."

Brie heard the sound of an electronic door bolt locking into place. She glanced around the room, staring at the colorful murals painted on the four walls. They were of different landscapes in Russia. Because they were life-like outdoor paintings, she'd never noticed that the room had no windows.

It suddenly dawned on her this was actually a panic room.

Tears sprang to her eyes when she realized Rytsar

had planned for this moment with the sole intention of protecting Hope. He knew there were those who might come for him seeking retribution.

Hope picked up on Brie's fear and cried out, squirming in her arms. Brie immediately smiled to calm her daughter and walked over to the white rocking horse. She helped Hope onto it. "Hold on tight."

She kept her tight smile, rubbing her pregnant belly while she slowly rocked the horse. Both she and Little Sparrow listened intently to the sounds of the men organizing on the other side of the door.

Suddenly, the air was filled with Rytsar's laughter.

Little Sparrow started dancing excitedly at the door.

In a matter of seconds, Brie heard the bolt being pulled back as the burly Russian, dressed and armed for battle, opened the door.

"There is nothing to fear, *radost moya.*"

Brie stared at him in disbelief, too stunned to speak.

"It seems your cavalry has arrived," he stated, petting Little Sparrow's head.

Brie shook her head in disbelief. "What?"

"The men you saw are here about your film."

"Mary did say it would happen soon," she said, laughing nervously. "But there are so many of them. I just assumed…"

Rytsar nodded. "As you should. You can never be too careful." He placed his hand on her shoulder, stating proudly, "It is time for you to meet your destiny."

He then glanced down at Hope. "*Vorobyshek* and I will watch the babe."

Brie looked at him in amazement. "I can't believe this is really happening…"

Picking up Hope, Rytsar escorted Brie out of the room. "Your Master wants you to return through the rear door."

Brie was humbled knowing Rystar and his men had mobilized to defend her and her daughter regardless of the cost. Deeply grateful to them, she smiled and nodded to each man as she walked past.

She headed back to the house and quietly entered through the back door where Sir was waiting for her. He wore an amused expression as he held out his arms to her.

Brie melted into his embrace. "Well, that was a scare…"

"An unnecessary one, at that," he agreed. "As punishment, I've made the men wait outside until you are ready."

She pulled back, her jaw dropping. "What? They're all outside?"

Sir nodded with a wicked glint in his eye. "Someone should have called you first."

Brie's heart started to race. "Do you think my mystery benefactor is out there right now?"

"I didn't recognize anyone, so I can't say."

She glanced nervously in the direction of the front door. "I'd better not keep them waiting."

"Actually, I want you to take your time to dress for this important meeting. They failed to inform you they were coming, so now they don't get the advantage of rushing you. Besides, it will take Mr. Thompson another forty minutes to arrive."

"You called our lawyer?"

He glanced at the front door. "There are a slew of

them out there, babygirl. No point in starting this meeting until you have proper representation."

Brie smiled up at him. "I'm grateful for your intervention, Sir."

He gazed down at her lovingly. "With Thompson by your side, you will be able to make a clear decision based on what is being offered."

"You aren't going to join me?" she asked in surprise.

He shook his head. "No. I don't want their attention to shift to me at any point during the meeting. They need to face the businesswoman behind the talent." He tucked a lock of her hair behind her ear. "You've earned this moment, Brianna Davis."

She nodded, feeling both humbled and empowered.

Brie headed to the bedroom. Understanding the significance of this meeting, she was determined to dress for it. She would have preferred wearing the red dress Sir had purchased for her months ago, but she was in her third trimester now and that wasn't an option for her.

Glancing at her round belly, Brie smiled. It was pretty amazing that she could grow a tiny human inside her while simultaneously advancing her film career.

Brie chose a white blouse and a stylish red jacket. Pulling her hair back in a severe ponytail, she smiled at her reflection. If they had any misconceptions that they were meeting a frumpy pregnant woman, they were entirely mistaken.

Brie was meticulous with her makeup and finished the look off with bright red lipstick. She pressed her lips together to gently blot the lipstick, then smiled at her reflection.

There was only one thing missing.

Brie walked to a drawer in the closet to get the white orchid comb. She wanted Tono to be a part of this momentous occasion. The Kinbaku Master had been with her in spirit every time she filmed, and she needed him to be with her now.

The moment she touched the flower, however, she felt a jolt of sadness. Brie realized that the last time she'd spoken to Tono was just before Kylie's death. Frowning in concern, she made a mental note to call him after the meeting.

Taking in a deep breath, she walked out of the bedroom and nodded to Sir. "I'm ready."

He looked at her with approval. "Yes, you certainly are."

Sir glanced at his watch. "Thompson texted and should be here any minute. I've set up the dining room table to act as your meeting room for today. Go ahead and sit down so you can settle in while I let them in."

"Thank you, Sir."

"Brie, if you need to address me at any point during the meeting, call me by my given name in their presence. I don't want them mistakenly thinking our unique dynamic influences what happens here today. This is your career, and I trust you to do what is best for your future."

Brie was moved by his unfailing belief in her. "You have always been supportive of my career."

He cupped her chin. "I am honored to be husband and Master of a gifted artist. I consider it a privilege." Kissing her on the lips, he winked as he added, "Prepare thyself, woman."

Brie grinned as she headed to the dining room. She

sat down at the head of the table and placed her palms on the smooth surface, surveying the rows of empty chairs that were about to be filled.

The butterflies started when she heard Sir invite the men inside. After being blacklisted by Holloway and watching everyone in the film industry turn their backs on her, her moment had finally come.

Her future was about to change.

Brie was anxious to meet the mysterious benefactor who had orchestrated this entire deal so she could thank him in person.

She stood up as the men filed in. "Please take a seat, gentlemen." She directed them, reserving the chair to her right for Mr. Thompson. The men each carried a briefcase and began rifling through them in silence while they waited.

Brie quietly observed them, scanning the room trying to determine which person was the mastermind behind all of this.

Mr. Thompson arrived a few minutes later, introducing her to another man he'd brought with him. "Mrs. Davis, I would like to introduce you to Henry Phillips. He is a highly regarded entertainment lawyer. I thought it best to have an expert in the field join us today."

Mr. Phillips held out his hand to Brie. "It is a pleasure to meet you, Mrs. Davis."

Shaking his hand firmly, she told him, "I appreciate any legal advice you have to offer, Mr. Phillips."

Brie addressed the man seated beside the empty chair reserved for Mr. Thompson. "I apologize for the inconvenience, but I will need you to make room for Mr. Phillips."

The man frowned but stood up, gesturing for Mr. Phillips to take his seat. There was a quick shuffle as the other men rearranged themselves around the table by some unknown ranking Brie was not privy to.

Once they were settled, Brie sat down again. "Now that everyone is here, let's begin."

The man to the left of her spoke up, "Mrs. Davis, you are aware we've come today with an offer to produce and distribute your latest documentary."

Brie smiled at him warmly. "And, your name is…"

"Randall Cummings, ma'am."

"Are you the man responsible for this offer?"

He cleared his throat. "No, Mrs. Davis."

She looked around the table. "Who is?"

Mr. Cummings explained, "We do not know the individual's identity, Mrs. Davis. We're simply here to make you the offer."

Brie frowned, tilting her head. "Why so many of you?"

"Each lawyer represents a client who will be involved in the production or distribution of your film."

Brie glanced around the table, humbled by the number of companies that would be involved.

"Let me begin by having the men introduce themselves and the clients they represent."

Brie sat in awe as each representative listed the top name in the industry he spoke for, from the famous film composer, and the first-class sound production team to the legendary Michael Schmidt, who was the greatest film editor in the business.

But it didn't end there…

A popular cinematographer had been hired for the

documentary to work on the transitions between each scene by creating breathtaking cutaway shots. Brie loved the idea because it would add a whole new dimension to the film.

Her documentary was not going to have one film distributor but many—each company specializing in their territory of the world. Not only that, but Brie learned they were scheduling it to release in theaters, DVD, cable, and digital download platforms.

This was the entire package!

Mr. Thompson went over each contract with an eagle eye while Mr. Phillips gave Brie a rundown on the individual businesses represented and further details about what was being provided by each entity.

"Collectively, this is a dream team," he whispered in her ear.

Brie nodded in agreement, thoroughly impressed. Looking at the army of men, she asked them, "So, let's get down to business. What is the actual offer?"

Mr. Cummings smiled. "I'm glad you asked."

He took a thick file from his briefcase and pushed it toward her. "Rather than a lump sum, the percentage reflects the funding required, as well as the considerable risk involved in assembling this unparalleled team."

Brie opened the folder and glanced at the first page. "I would receive ten percent of the net profit?"

"Yes, Mrs. Davis," Mr. Cummings replied without hesitation.

She nodded, then turned to her two lawyers. "I would like to discuss this privately with you."

"Certainly," Mr. Thompson answered.

"Gentlemen, if you'll excuse us," she stated, getting

up from the table. With as much grace as she could manage in her third trimester, Brie left the room with Mr. Thompson and Mr. Phillips following behind her.

She led them outside to discuss it with them while she watched the ocean waves breaking over the shore. "Do you feel this is a fair deal?"

"I do," Mr. Thompson replied.

"And you, Mr. Phillips?"

"It's quite generous considering there is no financial risk to you."

Brie nodded, her heart starting to race. This offer would allow countless people all over the world to see BDSM in a completely new light. That alone was worth it to her. But, having them offer her a dream team, along with considerable financial funding, made this deal suspect. It almost seemed too good to be true.

She asked Mr. Phillips, "Do you think it's strange that no one in the room knows who is actually financing the film?"

He nodded. "It is highly unusual, but then, so is your current situation with Holloway."

"Why would anyone agree to this, considering Holloway's influence in Hollywood?" she pressed him.

"The compensation must be considerable," Mr. Thompson stated frankly.

Mr. Phillips agreed. "Plus, there is power in numbers. The fact that the top echelon has agreed to work on this project protects them from being attacked individually by the man."

"Something concerns me," Brie confessed. "I have no idea who this person is or what vision they have for my film. While I appreciate having expert hands on my work, I don't want the essence of the message to be lost with all the changes being proposed."

"You should request the right for the final say," Mr. Phillips replied.

"Make it nonnegotiable," Mr. Thompson advised her. "But understand you may lose the offer if you do."

Brie nodded. Compromising the documentary was not an option for her. "So be it."

"You're sure?" Mr. Phillips insisted.

"Yes, as long as I retain control over the project, I'm onboard with everything."

Mr. Thompson grinned. "Are you ready to sign the contract, then?"

"I am, but I would like a moment to speak with Thane first."

While both men waited, Brie went to Sir's office to inform him of the offer and her decision.

"I think it is prudent to retain control," he told her.

"I'm glad you agree, Sir. I realize now I'd rather not have my documentary release than have the message muted by trying to make it more commercial with pretty bells and whistles—no matter who's involved in the project."

Sir pulled her to him and kissed her. "You impress me with the steadfast vision you have for your work."

"I'm glad you understand, Sir."

"Of course, I do. Leaving the message of your documentary in the hands of an unknown entity carries considerable risk. As you know, babygirl, I'm all about control."

She smiled, letting out an excited sigh. "Wish me luck, Sir!"

He winked. "Luck has nothing to do with this, baby-girl."

Oozing with confidence, Brie headed back to the table with Mr. Thompson and Mr. Phillips. While both men sat down beside her, Brie chose to remain standing.

Taking the time to look each man at the table in the eye, she told them, "I'm excited at the prospect of working with your clients on this project. However, I must retain the right of final say."

There was a collective gasp from the group.

"I cannot grant you that," Mr. Cummings stated. "I highly recommend you reconsider."

"If you can't add that to the contract, Mr. Cummings, then I suggest you speak to the person who can. As much as I appreciate this offer, it's nonnegotiable," she replied firmly.

Glancing at the other men, Mr. Cummings frowned and barked, "We are done here."

There was a flurry of activity as they picked up their contracts and thrusted them in their many briefcases while Brie watched in stunned silence.

Mr. Cummings stood up, handing her a piece of paper. "Please sign this."

Brie looked at the paper in confusion.

"It's a simple non-disclosure agreement," he stated.

She handed it to Mr. Thompson to look it over before signing it. After reading it, he told her, "It states that the terms stated in the offer, as well as clients represented, are confidential and will not be shared with any third party."

Brie nodded to him. "Fair enough."

"Mr. Davis will need to sign one, as well," Mr.

Cummings informed her, handing her another.

Mr. Thompson took the form. "I'll give this to Mr. Davis while you finish up here."

Brie signed the agreement, a queasy feeling washing over her. Instead of signing an offer, it felt as if she was signing away her future in film.

Although it was upsetting, Brie was grateful Mr. Holloway would never know the terms of the offer or the people in Hollywood who were brave enough to go against him.

Once Mr. Thompson returned with Sir's document, Mr. Cummings gave Brie a curt nod. "Good day, Mrs. Davis. I'm sorry for wasting your time."

The multitude of men filed out of the room with shocked expressions, clearly surprised she had turned down the unprecedented offer.

Brie turned to Mr. Thompson after they left and chuckled sadly. "I thought they would at least give it some consideration before withdrawing the offer."

Mr. Phillips stated, "Don't lose hope quite yet, Mrs. Davis. It's clear no one in attendance had the authority to make such a change."

Sir walked out of his office. "I'm sorry to hear the negotiation did not go well."

Brie looked at him forlornly, but instantly smiled when she heard the doorbell ring. Hurrying to answer it, Brie hoped it was Mr. Cummings wanting to renegotiate. Instead, she found Rytsar standing in the doorway with Hope in his arms looking at her expectantly. "Well, *radost moya?*"

She took Hope from him as she ushered Rytsar inside. Although she smiled, she was unable to hide her profound disappointment.

"What happened?" he asked in concern.

Trying to keep her answer light, she said in her best mobster voice, "Apparently, I made them an offer they *could* refuse."

Rytsar smirked. "Although I enjoy your sense of humor, *radost moya,* I don't understand."

She asked Mr. Thompson, "Can I tell him what I requested since it wasn't part of the original offer?"

"Certainly, Mrs. Davis."

Turning to Rytsar, she explained, "When I asked for final say over the film, they withdrew the offer."

Rytsar narrowed his eyes, pounding his fist against his palm. "Tell me who this person is so I can speak to them posthaste."

She let out a sad chuckle. "I still don't know. In fact, nobody who came to the meeting today claimed to know."

Brie held Hope up and twirled her around, saying with a tinge of regret, "It would have been amazing, sweet pea. The talent they amassed was beyond anything I could have dreamed of." She touched noses with Hope and added in a sing-song voice, "But that's the way the cookie crumbles."

The instant she set Hope down, Shadow appeared. Brie watched as her daughter toddled off to play with the big black cat, wonderfully unaware of the unfortunate turn of events that had just befallen her mother.

Brie mused, *Maybe it's for the best, with another baby on the way…*

Mr. Thompson held out his hand to Brie. "If they do reach out to you again, please don't hesitate to call."

Glancing at Phillips, he added, "We're both at your disposal, if you should need us."

"Thank you. Although it is not the outcome I wanted, I appreciated your counsel and do not regret my decision." She shook both their hands gratefully.

However—the idea that Holloway had won felt like a stab to Brie's heart.

His Promise

After the two men left, Brie found herself lightly fingering the white orchid in her hair.

"Are you okay, Brie?" Sir asked gently.

She turned to look at him and shook her head. "I feel the sudden need to speak to Tono, Sir. Do you mind if I call him?"

His eyes softened. "Not at all, babygirl."

"Tell the bondage Master to return to the States so he can tie up the person responsible for this while I *negotiate* a new offer..." Rytsar suggested.

Brie smiled. Having the sadistic Russian on her side made her disappointment easier to bear.

She retired to the bedroom and stared at the intricately painted wax form of her pregnant belly framed on the wall. Tono had made it for her when she was pregnant with Hope. That wax play scene with Tono was a cherished memory of hers and was preserved forever by this exquisite piece of art.

She dialed Tono's phone number, feeling an urgent need to connect with him.

As soon as he answered, she could tell something was wrong. "Is everything okay, Tono?"

He chuckled lightly, but she could hear the strain in his voice when he diverted her question by asking, "Are you well, Brie?"

"I…" She paused for a moment. Rather than answer him, she replied, "It's good to hear your voice."

"Yours, as well."

Tears pricked her eyes, wondering what he wasn't telling her. "I'm sorry I didn't call sooner, Tono."

There was a long moment of silence on the other end. "I'm sorry I wasn't there."

She felt her stomach twist. "You heard what happened to Kylie, then?"

"Marquis reached out to me."

Brie felt a sense of dread wash over her. She knew with certainty Tono would have flown back if he could. "Please tell me what's wrong."

Hearing his long sigh, she knew he was carefully picking his words. "I have had a…physical challenge to overcome."

Her bottom lip trembled. Her grief over Kylie had consumed her so completely that she'd never sensed his suffering. "I'm so sorry, Tono. Marquis never told—"

"I asked him to keep the news to himself, but I will share it with you now."

Brie clutched her phone as she quietly sank down on the bed.

"I'd been suffering from a debilitating headache for several weeks but I never had a fever, so I continued to work, not wanting to interrupt our international tour."

"What's wrong?" Brie whimpered, holding her

breath.

"It turns out I had strep but I didn't have any of the classic symptoms, so it went undiagnosed. It wasn't until Autumn came down with it that my doctor insisted on testing me."

When she heard it was only strep, Brie wanted to rejoice, but the tone in his voice terrified her. "What aren't you telling me?"

"Because it was left untreated, I developed glomeru-lonephritis. It's a disease that attacks the kidney."

Chills coursed through Brie knowing he had donated one kidney to Faelan. "Oh, Tono…"

His voice was gentle but firm. "I am fortunate to have an excellent medical staff overseeing my recovery and I am undergoing treatment right now to prevent further damage. If things continue to progress as they have been, I can return to my daily routine with only a few minor adjustments."

"Tono, I'm so scared for you…"

"Trust me. It's harder for those around me than it is for myself." He chuckled sadly. "Poor Autumn has suffered the most."

"I can only imagine," she whimpered.

"I'm in good hands, Brie," he assured her again. "Do not concern yourself with my welfare."

She cried, "You are asking for the impossible."

"Worry has no benefit," he chided her softly.

"Oh, Tono…" Her voice trailed off, the growing lump in her throat making it difficult to talk.

"Now you understand why I had Marquis Gray keep it from you—and Todd. The last thing Todd needs is to feel any guilt over this unfortunate situation."

Brie knew it would be devastating if Faelan learned that an undiagnosed condition had put Tono, the man who had donated a kidney to him, at risk.

After losing Kylie, it might prove too much for him to bear.

"I understand," she conceded, "but I wish I could rush to your side to help you and Autumn."

"We will see each other soon enough," he told her in his soothing voice. "Once I recover, and Autumn and I have finished out our tour, we will be free to return to the States."

"Do you think you'll be able to continue performing?" she asked with concern.

"It is my goal and my main focus."

Brie sighed, feeling unsettled. "I hate that we are so far away."

"Not in spirit," Tono reminded her. "And I know I'm not the only one who has been suffering."

Her voice caught when she thought about Kylie. "Yes…" Suddenly, the pain of her death, coupled with the disappointment of the film and this frightening news about Tono, overwhelmed her and she fell mute.

"Brie."

The lump in her throat became painful, making it impossible to answer him.

"Toriko…"

The warmth that flowed from his voice filled her with a sudden sense of calm and wellbeing.

"Talk to me," he insisted gently.

Brie shook her head even though he couldn't see it. "You're sick, Tono."

"I told you my situation. Now, it is your turn to tell

She hesitated but gave in to his quiet command. “I’m still grieving Kylie’s death and watching Faelan’s soul waste away…it has eaten at my heart.”

“I am deeply troubled that I cannot be there for either of you.” Tono’s voice was heavy with regret. “But something spurred you to call me today. I can feel it.”

Brie groaned, knowing she could never hide anything from Tono. “It’s not a matter of life or death—”

“Tell me.”

She sighed softly. “I thought I had an offer for the second documentary. I even put your flower in my hair before the meeting started. What they offered was beyond my wildest dreams, Tono, and I had my heart set on it. But…” Her voice faltered. “I asked for final say over the project and they immediately turned me down.”

“I can feel your disappointment from here. However, you know in your heart you were right.”

“I do…” she agreed miserably. A sob escaped her lips when she confessed, “But Holloway won.”

“No,” Tono stated firmly.

Tears welled up in her eyes wanting desperately to believe him.

“That malevolent husk of a being does *not* own your future.”

Tono said it with such force, it felt as if she’d been hit in the chest. It took her a few moments to realize she’d been holding her breath.

“Do you hear me?”

“Yes, Tono.”

“Continue on your path and do not waver from it. I vow to do the same.”

His promise filled Brie with hope. It was as if their invisible bond had grown stronger and was powerful enough to propel them both forward.

"You fill my heart with joy, Tono."

"Even in your suffering, you are a strength to me," he replied.

She laughed softly. "No. It's the other way around."

Understanding the immense fear Autumn must be experiencing because of Tono's health, Brie asked him, "Where are you now?"

"A hospital in Seoul, Korea."

Brie's stomach dropped. The seriousness of his condition hit her all over again. "Do you have an address where I can send something to Autumn?"

"She would appreciate that. I'll text it to you after our call. I asked Autumn to keep my condition from everyone for fear of the news finding its way to Todd. Unfortunately, in doing so, she has been deprived of the support she needs."

"Am I allowed to tell Sir about this?"

"Of course."

Wanting to give Tono a ray of hope, she told him, "You should know Faelan is leaving with Rytsar for Russia."

"What about the child?"

"Grace is going to remain under Marquis and Celestia's care. Rytsar is convinced he can help Faelan through this, and I am trusting with all of my heart that he can."

"So, he named the baby Grace?"

"Not exactly..." she answered. "Faelan never officially named his daughter, but Celestia pressed him for one before leaving. He told her to call the baby Grace

21

for the time being, because they both need it."

Tono grunted in pain.

"Are you okay?" Brie whimpered.

"It hurts my soul, knowing the pain he and the child are suffering."

"Yes…"

"Please keep me updated. If there is a need and I can travel, I will come."

"Right now, you must heal, Tono. It's the only thing Faelan needs from you," she said with conviction.

Brie could hear the smile in his voice when he asked, "Are you giving me a command?"

She grinned into the phone. "Only in the most respectful manner."

Waves of pure joy coursed through her spirit when she heard his laughter.

"Take care of yourself. Before you know it, there will be a second member of the Davis household for you to look after."

"I have almost two months left, which I know doesn't sound like a lot. But when you're in the last trimester, it becomes the longest two months of your life."

He chuckled. "I will have to take your word for it."

"Tono…" Brie hated to let him go, but she didn't want to overtax him. "I long for the day when I see you in person." The lump in her throat returned.

"I live for that day," he assured her.

Brie swallowed hard. "Please give Autumn my love. I'm not going to say goodbye—just see you soon."

"See you soon, Brie," he replied warmly. "Give Sir Davis my best and tell him not to second guess himself."

Brie hung up, unsure what he meant by that last statement. She stared at the cell phone, her emotions all over the place. However, she clung to the feeling of calm talking to Tono always inspired.

Getting up from the bed, she went to rejoin Sir and Rytsar.

The instant Sir saw Brie, he asked, "Is Nosaka okay?"

When she shook her head, he walked over and put his arms around her.

Staring up into his troubled eyes, she quickly added, "But he will be."

Sir guided her to the couch as she explained what happened to Tono. "It's terrifying to think we might have lost—" She couldn't even bring herself to say it out loud.

When Brie looked into Sir's tormented eyes, she realized he was gripped by a sense of responsibility having helped to make the organ match between Tono and Faelan.

Tono's words suddenly replayed in her head, so she assured Sir, "Tono has no regrets. He specifically told me you shouldn't second guess yourself."

Sir shook his head with a sad smile. "Nosaka knows me a little *too* well."

"Is there any way I can help, *radost moya*?" Rytsar asked.

"You already are. Tono is deeply concerned about Faelan, but knowing you are handling the situation gives him peace he would not have had otherwise."

"I will do right by the boy," Rytsar vowed.

"I have every confidence you will."

"Did Nosaka say anything about your offer being

turned down?" Sir asked, knowing how invested Tono was in her film career.

"He insisted it doesn't change anything."

Sir nodded his approval, then leaned down to kiss her on the lips. "I concur."

Brie smiled up at Sir, his strength and vitality a commanding force that comforted her.

"You know…" Rytsar began with a wicked glint in his eyes, "I was supposed to be on a flight to Russia by now, but due to today's unexpected events, I won't be leaving until tomorrow."

He nodded to Sir. "*Moy droog*, why don't you play hooky? We'll tucker *moye solntse* out by splashing in the ocean and then turn our intentions on *radost moya* once the babe is down for her nap."

"I do think téa and I would benefit from a creative expenditure of energy after this unwarranted sneak attack."

Brie nodded thoughtfully. "Attack…that's exactly how it felt when they arrived."

"I believe there was a purpose behind its execution," Sir stated firmly. "Their intent was to shock and awe, so you wouldn't question the offer." He smiled at her with pride. "However, they failed to appreciate you are a businesswoman who will not be rattled by such underhanded tactics."

"The way it was handled was not only offensive but entirely unnecessary," Rytsar growled.

"The more I think about it, the happier I am that I turned the offer down." Brie lifted her chin up in defiance. "I refuse to be treated like a pawn."

"Of course, not—when you are the queen," Sir

agreed, kissing her on the lips.

Brie sighed in contentment. Picking up Hope, she headed to the nursery to change her. She was excited about the unexpected outing.

It truly amazed her that in less than an hour, she'd gone from being terrified and profoundly disappointed, to feeling empowered about her future.

That was the power of being surrounded by good people—they kept your eyes on the bigger picture while reminding you of what really matters.

Connection

Her heart lighter, Brie dressed Hope up in a cute little one-piece swimsuit with a big sunflower on the tummy.

When she went downstairs, Rytsar took Hope from her arms, growling like a Kodiak bear. "Are you ready to play in the ocean, *moye solntse?*"

Sir appeared from the bedroom carrying beach towels, dressed in only his swim trunks. "I laid out your swimsuit for you. Meet the three of us outside."

She couldn't help gazing at his toned chest covered in dark hair. Everything about Sir's body called to her as a woman.

After getting dressed in the purple swimsuit Sir had chosen for her, Brie met them on the beach. Rytsar was already in the water with Hope, playing in the waves. Brie smiled when she heard her daughter squealing in Rytsar's arms as the waves crashed around them.

"Ready for a dip in the ocean?" Without waiting for a response, Sir surprised Brie by sweeping her up in his arms and heading to the water.

"Oh, no! Put me down, put me down…" she giggled, worried she was too heavy for him.

He looked down at her and smirked. "No."

Brie instantly stopped resisting as he carried her into the ocean. In a world of disappointments and fear, the magic of the ocean was its power to erase all the negativity she was experiencing—if only for a moment.

It brought balance to Brie's soul.

She felt like a kid again hearing Sir laugh when they were hit by a big wave. They were both drenched by it, but Sir held her tight, not letting go until they were far enough out for Brie to float on each swell.

The four of them stayed in the water for a long time, the two men taking turns playing with Hope while Brie gently rolled with the surges. The beauty of the ocean was the temporary freedom from gravity that it gave her pregnant body.

They lay on the sand afterwards in thoughtful silence, listening to the peaceful sound of the waves.

When Hope let out a big yawn, Brie took it as her cue that it was time for a nap. Rytsar insisted on tucking Hope in for her nap, stating, "I do not know when I will be back again."

Brie could feel his sadness as she watched Rytsar carry Hope upstairs. The pain of a *dyadya* was real.

When he didn't come back after several minutes, curiosity got the best of Brie and she snuck up to see what he was doing. She heard his low voice coming from the room. He was singing the Russian lullaby that his mother used to sing to him—his deep, masculine voice resonating in Brie's soul.

Hope stared up at Rytsar, transfixed.

Brie hated that Hope was facing the loss of her *dy-adya* again. It was unfair, and it had everything to do with Lilly.

Brie hoped there would come a day when Rytsar would not have to sacrifice himself because of that evil woman—that someday, their lives would not be controlled by her.

Until then, Rytsar would stand as Hope's protector, making sure no one ever hurt his *moye solntse*.

After he shut the door to the nursery, Rytsar told Brie, "I hope she does not forget me."

"I won't let her, Rytsar," Brie promised.

The burly Russian looked away for a moment to swipe a tear from his eye. When he turned back to her, he smiled. "Now, I get to enjoy a second goodbye with you. It is an unforeseen luxury."

Her heart fluttered.

When they entered the bedroom, Sir was already showered and waiting for them. "What is your instrument of choice, old friend?"

Rytsar looked Brie over and cocked his head. "No need for a formal instrument. I am going to use the traditional tool of a Russian." He leaned over and whispered in Sir's ear.

Brie shivered anxiously, wondering what the sadist had in store for her.

"While I get the needed item, why don't the two of you rinse off?" Sir suggested.

Rytsar placed his hand on the back of Brie's neck and squeezed. It instantly sent chills through her body, making her feel like a helpless kitten.

Escorting her to the bathroom, Rytsar reached into

the Roman shower to turn on the water. While it ran, Rytsar quickly stripped out of his swim trunks and then helped Brie out of her bathing suit.

Once she was free of the wet material, he commanded she join him. He scrubbed every part of her body with luxurious suds. Then he used her body as his personal sponge, rubbing his body against hers. It was a sensual exchange of suds.

Once he was satisfied, Rytsar turned both shower-heads on full blast so they were drenched in hot water. It guaranteed that there would be no grain of sand left after he toweled her off, but it left her feeling like a drowned cat.

Rubbing her thoroughly, he was as methodical drying her off as he had been lathering her up. Her skin quickly got pink under his intense care. When it came time to dry her hair, he used the towel like he was drying off Little Sparrow after a bath, leaving Brie's hair a tousled mess.

Rytsar smirked at her when he picked up her golden paddle brush.

Sir walked into the bathroom carrying an ice bucket.

Brie's eyes widened when she realized what Rytsar had planned for her after their hot shower together.

Handing the brush to Sir, he stated huskily, "See to her hair while I tend to her arousal."

Brie dutifully sat down on the bench Sir slid to the middle of the bathroom. Where Rytsar's hands had been rough, Sir's were gentle as he took on the challenge of carefully brushing out the wet tangles the Russian had created.

She basked in his soothing touch as he patiently

brushed through her hair, creating a cascade of sensual tingles from her head down to her toes.

Naturally, that's when Rytsar kicked things up a notch.

Brie let out a little squeak when he slid an ice cube against her warm skin. "*Da…*" he growled hungrily, satisfied with her reaction.

She bit her lip, trying to hold back her squeals as he used those ice cubes in the most indecent ways, beginning with every inch of her skin before moving to every orifice. By the time he was done, she was sitting in a puddle of water, goosebumps covering her entire body.

"Welcome to Russia!" he chuckled as he leaned down to kiss her.

The ache of the cold instantly flared into desire when he claimed her mouth. The heat of his tongue was a sharp contrast to the coolness of her mouth, causing them both to moan.

When Rytsar finally broke the embrace, Sir helped Brie up and guided her to the bed. With her entire body trembling from Rytsar's icy attention, Brie whimpered in excitement as the two men lay down on either side of her and began devouring her—licking and nibbling her chilled skin.

"I need to dive into that frigid ass," Rytsar growled huskily.

Brie enjoyed the humor behind his statement and watched in anticipation as he coated his hard cock with lubricant.

Sir distracted her by taking a piece of ice and placing it in his mouth before leaning down to kiss her. She moaned as she parted her lips and they shared the ice between them. The act was so sensual and intimate that Brie willingly invited the chill that coursed through her body.

When Sir pulled away, the ravenous look in his eyes gave her butterflies.

"Kneel on all fours, téa."

Too far along in her pregnancy to take both men at the same time, Sir piled pillows to support her upper torso. He joined her on the bed and fisted her hair, pulling her head back. "I've always enjoyed watching my cock disappear down your throat."

Sir groaned in pleasure when she parted her cold lips for him. Brie eagerly took his shaft, relaxing her throat to take the fullness of his cock.

Brie felt Rytsar settle on the bed behind her. Her stomach fluttered as he spread her ass cheeks and pressed his warm shaft against her cold rosette.

"I'll go slow, *radost moya*. I wouldn't want you to harm my comrade's manhood with those teeth."

"How thoughtful of you, old friend…" Sir muttered, pushing his cock farther down her throat.

Brie closed her eyes as Rytsar's cock invaded her icy depths. His shaft felt so hot that she whimpered around her Master's shaft in surprise.

Sir immediately pulled out. "Color, téa?"

"Green, Master," she assured him.

She looked back toward Rytsar. "You're like fire!"

The Russian's low chuckle filled the air as he slapped her ass before continuing his sensual invasion.

Brie turned back to Sir, purring, "I'm hungry to please you, Master."

The two men took their time, their strokes slow,

measured, and ever-deepening. There was a primal satisfaction in pleasing both men. It filled Brie with a profound sense of feminine power.

Before long, the friction of their bodies began to warm her from the inside out. The men took turns, Rytsar holding still, his shaft buried deep in her ass while Sir pumped his cock into her mouth. Then Sir would stop and command her to slowly stroke his shaft with her hand while Rytsar had his way with her. It went on and on, the momentary breaks giving each man more stamina.

As for Brie, she was in pure submissive heaven…

When the two Doms were close to orgasm, Sir broke away from Brie and stroked himself while Rytsar vigorously fingered her clit. Watching Sir was sexy as hell—but having Rytsar play with her at the same time took it to a whole new level.

When Sir was ready, he commanded, "Open for me, téa."

Brie eagerly parted her lips while Rytsar pushed himself deeper into her ass.

Her pussy was pulsing with need when she felt the men tense just before climaxing. Their lusty groans filled the air as both men released inside her. It took Brie over the edge and her pussy began contracting as she joined them in climax.

Both Doms lay on either side of her afterward, the three of them basking in satisfied silence. If Brie could have had her way, she would have spent the rest of the day like this.

However, Sir got up and started dressing. "Why don't you finish with her aftercare while I prepare for the afternoon meeting I have scheduled today?"

Clutching Brie to him, Rytsar tsked in mock disgust. "Such is the sad life of a peasant."

Sir chuckled. "I wouldn't have it any other way."

He then glanced at Brie and smiled. "Enjoy this time, babygirl. No need to rush it."

Brie looked at him lovingly. "Thank you, Sir."

After he left, Rytsar commanded Brie to lie back down. He ran his hand over her entire body, stating, "It amazes me that your body is so perfect, *radost moya.*"

She snorted in amusement, feeling anything but perfect at this stage of her pregnancy.

The harsh look Rytsar gave her instantly silenced Brie.

"As I was saying…" he continued, grazing his fingers lightly over her skin. "Everything about you pleases me."

She gazed into his piercing blue eyes, deeply touched by his words.

Running his fingers down her arm, he stopped at her elbow. "How is it that even your elbow turns me on?"

She smirked.

Raising his eyebrows, he stated, "You don't believe me?" He glanced down at his crotch for emphasis.

Brie followed his gaze and was surprised to see he was already growing hard again. "It may be your incredible libido rather than my elbow."

He shook his head slowly, his gaze intense.

Brie dared not contradict the sadist, but asked in a playful tone, "What about my swollen ankles?"

He smirked, his hands slowly traveling down to caress them. "They are even more arousing to me, knowing that the babe growing in your belly is the reason for it."

Brie held her breath as he kissed her left ankle tenderly before nipping it. When she squirmed, he held her ankle tightly and kissed it again before moving to the other.

Tears welled up in her eyes, amazed at how he could make her feel so loved.

Rytsar glanced down at his shaft, which had grown more rigid.

She giggled. "Surely there is something about my body you don't find attractive."

With a look of determination, he examined every part of her body with embarrassing thoroughness, flipping her from side to side so no inch of skin, no crevice, was left untouched.

"*Nyet*. There is not," he finally answered. "You are fully and wholly pleasing to me." His shaft was now rock hard after his thorough examination.

Brie blushed under the force of his gaze and high praise. "How may I please you further?"

Rytsar took her hand and placed it on his cock. "Your Master and I have an unspoken agreement. I will never claim you when we are alone unless there is a prior arrangement."

Brie thought back to the time Sir had given Rytsar permission to couple with Brie just before the Koslov brothers captured him and dragged him to Russia. It had been such an achingly sweet moment when the burly Russian made tender love to his Tatianna vicariously through Brie.

She stared into Rytsar's blue eyes as she tightened her grip around his cock and began stroking him slowly. He groaned in satisfaction as he lay on the bed, propping his head with his hand so he could stare at her while she played with him.

Her aim was not to build him up for a quick release but to make love to his cock using only her touch. Brie needed him to know the depth of her feelings, especially with him leaving for Russia tomorrow.

She held his shaft tighter as she moved up and down the length of it, twisting her wrist each time she reached the head of his cock. Brie varied the speed and firmness of her grasp, her eyes never breaking his gaze.

Soon, her fingers were slippery with his precome.

Brie used it to increase the intensity of her sensual caress while still being careful not to take the Russian over the edge.

"Tighter," he growled huskily.

She tightened her grip but slowed her strokes considerably.

He shook his head and smirked, obviously enjoying her focused attention but fighting to maintain control.

"Do you know, *radost moya*, that last night with you was the first time I ever willingly offered myself to a woman?"

Brie was about to reply when he placed his finger on her lips. Her heart began to race as he continued. "I have never wanted to before. Could never imagine myself doing such a thing as a Dominant…" His voice trailed off and he was silent for a moment.

Brie continued to stroke him, her love growing for the man.

"In retrospect, I find it interesting that I needed the safety of our threesome despite the fact I trust you with my life."

She looked at him with understanding. Brie knew about the betrayal and violation he'd suffered under the hands of Ms. Clark many years ago.

Rytsar's eyes softened when he added, "I suppose I needed to test that boundary with you. But, I have no idea why."

She crinkled her brow in concern.

"What?" he asked. "You have permission to speak."

"Do you regret last night, Rytsar?"

A slow smile spread across his face. "*Nyet.*"

He pulled her to him. "I feel closer to you now." He kissed her then, his fingers finding their way between her legs. Brie moaned in pleasure, her body fully in tune with his as he explored her mouth with his tongue.

Wanting to ride this crest of ecstasy with him, Brie grabbed his cock and began stroking him again. Brie lost herself when he claimed her mouth.

She felt him tense just moments before he groaned deeply. Her orgasm followed the moment she felt his warm seed on her belly. It was so erotic, she thought she might burst into flame from the heat of it.

Afterward, they both lay together in comfortable silence.

Rytsar surprised her when he started chuckling.

She grinned. "What's so funny?"

"I was just thinking back on your little prank. Would you like to know how it played out?"

Brie blushed—she knew there was no point in denying she had a hand in it—and nodded eagerly.

"Just minutes after arriving at the beach house, after weeks of being gone, one of my men sat down on a barstool at the kitchen counter. We had no idea what we were in for until the smell of the bomb wafted through the kitchen. My man quickly located the source and picked it up, then opened the trashcan, which naturally triggered another bomb.

"We opened all the windows and doors to let the kitchen air out, but the smell was too obnoxious. I went to grab a bottle of vodka…and that's when I tripped the next little nugget of putridness."

He chuckled ruefully. "I was cursing Anderson the entire time as I had my men scour the place. There was no way to disarm the booby traps, so my men and I were forced to scurry about, trying to throw the bombs outside before they exploded."

Brie could just imagine and tried hard not to laugh.

"It took us almost an hour to locate and rid my house of all those vile things."

Brie covered her mouth, her eyes wide with amusement when he told her, "I did not realize my mistake until I sat down on the toilet. The instant I heard the telltale sound of the bomb inflating I knew my fate was sealed…"

He raised an eyebrow, looking at her accusingly. "Needless to say, in my compromised position, I only had time to throw the damn thing in my bathtub and throw a towel over it."

Rytsar shook his head slowly. "That obnoxious smell lasted for days, *radost moya*. Days!"

She let out a little squeak, loving his recounting way too much.

"My men and I scanned the entire house two more times before I was confident we'd located them all.

"But…" he growled ominously. "I had not counted

on my boots buried in the back of the closet."

Brie bit her lip, trying desperately not to laugh.

"Master Anderson may have been the brains behind the sneak attack, but it was your simple but effective touches that truly made this deadly."

Brie couldn't hold it back any longer and started to laugh. "I'm so sorry, Rytsar."

He smirked. "*Nyet.* You are not."

She burst out in a full-on belly laugh, imagining the sexy Russian and all of those deadly bodyguards running in sheer terror just like she had, hoping to get the little silver packets with yellow smiley faces out of the house before detonation.

It was priceless!

"Do you forgive me?"

He snorted. "Do you forgive me for returning the favor?"

Brie giggled, telling him how she had unwittingly flashed one of their neighbors as she tried to get rid of the thing. She grinned afterward. "I loved it."

"As did I, *radost moya*..." His low chuckle filled the room. He nuzzled her neck before biting down on her delicate skin, sending delightful shivers down her spine.

Send-Off

The following day, Brie went with Sir to see Rytsar and Faelan off. She'd left Hope with her parents out of concern for Faelan, uncertain how he was handling his grief over Kylie now that he intended to leave for Russia with Rytsar.

Marquis Gray answered the door and nodded respectfully to the Russian before addressing Sir and Brie, "It is good you two came as well."

Brie held her breath as Marquis Gray ushered them into the house. She had hoped to see an improvement in Faelan but, as soon as they entered the room, she was disheartened to see he was even more pale and gaunt than before.

"Are you ready for this?" Rytsar asked him.

Faelan glanced in their direction, the grief in his eyes so palpable that Brie gasped in pain.

Celestia walked into the room, carrying the crying child. Brie wondered if the little girl could sense Faelan was leaving her. The desperate sound of the baby's wails broke her heart.

Faelan winced and closed his eyes. "The sooner we do this, the better."

Sir picked up the suitcase in the hallway while Rytsar slapped Faelan soundly on the back. "It will get better."

Faelan let out a low grunt as if he didn't believe Rytsar. He then turned to Marquis and Celestia and frowned. "I'm sorry for the burden I have become."

"You are not a burden," Marquis stated firmly.

Glancing briefly at the bereft child in Celestia's arms, Faelan said with regret, "It's unfair of me to ask this of you."

Celestia was quick to answer. "We do this out of love for you both, Todd."

Marquis clasped his shoulder. "Do what you must to reground yourself for your daughter. She deserves no less from you."

Faelan nodded curtly and turned to leave.

The child's cries intensified when he walked away. Brie held her breath, her heart aching for his little girl.

Faelan suddenly stopped in his tracks and walked back to his daughter, holding out his hands. Celestia placed the crying baby in his arms.

He cradled her against his chest and gently hushed her. The tiny baby quieted, then looked up at him with teary eyes.

"I will come back for you. I promise." Faelan kissed her on the forehead before handing her back to Celestia.

Brie saw Faelan swipe his eye as he rushed out of the room without looking back. Following quietly behind Sir, Brie listened as the child began to wail again.

Once outside, it crushed her when Faelan stared up at the sky and said, "I'm barely hanging on by a thread,

Kylie."

"Do not look back, only forward," Rytsar stated gruffly as they walked to the vehicle.

Sir handed the suitcase to Rytsar's man and stood beside Brie, wrapping his arm around her. "If you need anything, Wallace, don't hesitate to call Brie and I."

Faelan held out his hand to Sir. "You helped saved my life once. I'd prefer not to owe you a second time."

Brie instantly thought of Tono and struggled not to show any emotion when Faelan gazed into her eyes. "Look after Celestia for me, blossom. I don't know how long this will take and she'll have her hands full with my little girl."

"I will."

Faelan suddenly frowned and looked away. "I can't imagine life without Kylie. I don't even want to…"

"I know," Brie whimpered.

When Faelan met her gaze again, she was hit by the immensity of his grief. "Life means nothing without her, blossom."

She took his hand and squeezed it. "But you'll find a way."

Faelan glanced toward the house briefly, before turning to Rytsar. "You'll live to regret letting me tag along with you."

Rytsar snorted. "You're wrong. I am a man who no longer lives with regret."

Brie felt chills, moved by the profound truth behind his words.

With Sir by her side, she watched Faelan get in the vehicle. He called for Little Sparrow, who jumped in to join him.

Rytsar nodded to Brie. "He will be a changed man on our return, *radost moya*."

"I'm grateful…for everything." She swallowed hard to keep her emotions in check.

Rytsar winked at her. "There is nothing I'd rather do than ensure the creature is no longer a threat to you."

"You'll keep us apprised of the situation?" Sir asked him.

"Of course, *moy droog*."

Sir furrowed his brow and looked at Rytsar thoughtfully. "I hope to repay you for helping with my sister."

"*Nyet*."

Leaning toward him, Brie heard Rytsar whisper, "I do this for me as much as for you, comrade."

As Brie watched them drive away, she felt a great emptiness in their wake.

Once they were out of sight, Sir guided Brie back inside. They were greeted by the loud wails of the little baby. Brie immediately went to relieve Celestia. "Let me hold this little bundle of sad cuteness."

"Celestia," Marquis asked, "would you brew us some chamomile tea and bring a cup for yourself? We could all use a moment of calm."

After she left, Marquis addressed Sir. "I know it is not my place, and you are within your right to say no, but I would like to be kept informed on how things progress in Russia."

Brie was certain Marquis was speaking about Lilly and wondered how Sir would respond to his request. Even though Sir had found a solution Marquis approved of, there was no mistaking that the trainer remained concerned about Lilly's welfare.

Sir stared at Marquis for a long time before answering. "When I have news worth sharing, I will make a point of letting you know."

Marquis nodded.

Celestia returned, carrying a tray. With grace and a sense of formality, she poured the tea and handed the first cup to her Master. She then handed one to Sir and then poured the next cup for Brie.

Bouncing the crying child in her arms, Brie told her, "No, sit down and enjoy the tea while it's still hot. Grace and I are getting reacquainted."

Celestia smiled and did as Brie asked, but never took her eyes off the child as she sat and sipped her tea.

Brie noticed Marquis quietly observing his submissive.

The moment Celestia got up to pour him more tea, he stopped her. "Rather than another cup of tea, I would find a flogging session more relaxing."

Celestia looked at him with pleading eyes, clearly needing that release. "Yes, Master."

Glancing at Sir, Marquis asked, "Would you mind caring for the child while we take a few minutes to ourselves?"

"Take as much time as you need. In fact, we could take her home with us if you'd like."

Celestia's concerned gaze darted toward the baby.

"No, that is unnecessary," Marquis assured him. "The child has suffered enough separation for one day."

Turning to Celestia, he held out his hand to her. "Come with me, my love."

Celestia took his hand, a little gasp escaping her lips as he lifted her to her feet.

"It has been far too long," he murmured as he escorted her out of the room.

Brie felt immense joy as she watched them walk out of the room together.

"They have a tough road ahead," Sir stated once they were gone.

Brie looked down at the unhappy child. "I wish I could let Grace know it's going to be okay."

Sir stared at the crying child with a troubled expression. "These next few months are going to be difficult, but she is not the only one I worry about. It's important that Marquis and Celestia look after themselves, as well."

Brie perked up. "I know your aunt and uncle have offered to babysit, and I would be happy to help."

He leaned down and kissed her on the cheek, laying his hand on her pregnant belly. "You need to take care of yourself and our own little girl."

Brie stared up at him, loving how Sir looked out for everyone—especially her. "I know Mary has a long list of people who want to help."

"Excellent. I'll speak to Miss Wilson and see if we can't schedule a rotation of people. Knowing Gray, it's not something he would consider asking for himself."

Even with a wailing infant in her arms, Brie was overwhelmed by the beauty of this moment. "I love everything about you, Sir."

He smirked. "Foolish sub…"

Taking the baby from her, he told her, "Let's go on a long walk so Celestia can concentrate on her Master rather than a crying child."

Brie walked the neighborhood beside Sir, moved beyond words by his thoughtfulness. Her heart was so full of love for the man, she felt like she might burst.

Knowing how emotionally invested Mary was in the success of the second documentary, Brie called her when they arrived home hours later and let her know about the failed negotiations.

Brie had secretly held onto the hope that Mr. Cummings would return with an updated contract the next day, making this call unnecessary. Unfortunately, that hadn't happened, and Brie didn't want Mary to hear about it from anyone else.

"What's up, Stinks? Got some fabulous news to tell me? You're welcome, by the way."

She answered truthfully, "I appreciate everything you've done, Mary."

"Wait! Something's wrong…I can hear it in your voice. What happened?"

Brie let out an anguished sigh.

"They contacted you with an offer, right?"

"They did."

"Did they insult you with a shit deal?" she growled angrily. "Those mother fuckers…"

"Not exactly."

Mary was silent for a moment. "What did they offer you?"

"I can't say."

"What the hell, bitch? I deserve better than that from you!"

"You do, but I signed a confidentiality agreement."

"Fuck!" Mary snarled. "I know you can't say who it is, but did you at least meet the person behind all this?"

"No. I still have no idea who it is."

Mary huffed. "Are you telling me this was all some fucking ruse?"

"No, I believe the offer was genuine. In fact, it was a good one."

Mary demanded, "Why didn't you take it, damn it."

"There was one issue I couldn't ignore."

"Let me guess…you can't tell me what that is," Mary snarled.

"Actually, my lawyer said I can."

"Well? Spit it out."

Brie sighed heavily, reliving the shock and disappointment. "I asked for final say over the film and they all walked out."

Her confession was met with silence.

Aware of all the sacrifices Mary had made trying to make this offer a reality, despite Holloway's displeasure, Brie was prepared for an ugly tongue-lashing.

Instead, Mary laughed. "Damn it, Stinks…I couldn't be prouder of you than I am right now."

Brie snorted in disbelief. "Really?"

"Absolutely. You have no idea who's behind this or what their motives are. Why trust your documentary and reputation to someone who won't even show their face to you?"

Brie was touched by Mary's reaction. "After all you've been through…everything you've risked for me, I thought—" She cleared her throat, her emotions suddenly getting the best of her. "You never cease to amaze me, Mary."

"I hope you know I would have throat punched you had you agreed to that deal."

Brie burst out laughing. "Now, that's the Mary I know and love."

"So, what's the plan now, Stinks?"

"I'm going to continue making my next documentary. Holloway has no power over my future. Tono said so himself."

"Oh, so you've been talking to the rope Master, have you?"

Knowing Mary was currently living with Lea to avoid Holloway's wrath, Brie immediately changed the subject to avoid exposing the secret of Tono's health. Lowering her voice, she asked, "I need to know something."

Mary immediately replied in a snarky tone, "You can ask, bitch. But that doesn't mean I'll answer you."

Brie frowned, worried about her. "Now that we know there is no other offer coming, what are your plans?"

Mary's voice suddenly became cold and defensive. "What do you mean?"

Brie was afraid this was the reaction she would get, but forged ahead anyway, "With Greg Holloway."

Brie could feel the tension building when Mary snarled, "What about him?"

"Are you going to finally dump the creep?"

She burst out laughing as if the question were absurd. "Once Greg hears the offer fell through, he'll want me by his side so he can gloat every chance he gets. There's no getting out of this."

"Mary, just say the word," Brie begged. "You have a team of people that can help you get away from the bastard."

Her voice gave Brie chills. "I don't think you understand, Brie. Now that the threat of the offer no longer exists, Holloway will be even more powerful than he was before. Things are about to get real ugly."

"Then you have to get away now!"

"You have it all wrong. Without me there, you will pay in ways you could never imagine. You think Greg will stand by and let you go on your merry way as if nothing happened?"

"Mary, I—"

"I knew this was a possibility, Brie. My eyes were wide open when I made the decision to help you. I don't regret it—not for a second."

A lump formed in Brie's throat. "You don't have to accept this as your fate."

Mary let out an exasperated sigh. "Don't you get it? Without me on the front lines, your future is forfeit. You have no idea the lengths Greg will go to make you and your family pay for this failed coup. Oh, wait..." She laughed sarcastically. "Actually, you do. But I guarantee, what he did to me and my mother will pale in comparison to what he'll do to you—unless I'm there to stop it."

Ice ran through Brie's veins when she heard Mary's assertion. Remembering Tono's words about Holloway's effect on her future, she said confidently, "I refuse to believe that."

"Fine. It's better if you don't. But I know the truth, Brie. So let me do what I have to do."

"No, I can't let you sacrifice yourself."

Her laughter was harsh. "I'm the whole reason you're entangled with the bastard, so I'm committed to doing whatever it takes to protect you from his wrath."

"But, Mary—"

"Don't worry about me. He'll gloat for a couple of months, do his best to humiliate me in front of his friends. Hell…if I play him right, it won't be long before he'll get tired and move on to some new conquest of his. You were just a means to an end, Stinks. As long as I'm there to distract him, he won't need to torment you."

"I won't let you do that!" Brie cried.

Mary's voice became ice cold. "This is my life, bitch. Nobody gets to control what I do—not even you."

"I'm not okay with this plan, Mary."

The tone in her voice grew more hostile. "This isn't up for debate, and if you talk to *anyone* about it, I'll jump down the rabbit hole so fast, it will make your head spin."

Brie had no idea what she meant, but it terrified her.

Although she knew Mary's actions came from a place of love, because of her violent past, the way she expressed it was dark and twisted—and Brie wasn't sure if Mary would survive it.

"You *better* not betray me, bitch," Mary warned, her voice full of venom.

Brie heard a rapping knock in the background, followed by Lea's cheerful voice. "Hey, just a heads up. Hunter's going to be here in a few."

"Oh, yay!" Mary answered in a sarcastic tone.

Mary lowered her voice and whispered into the phone so only Brie could hear, "At least now I don't have a reason to stay here anymore."

"Who are you talking to?" Lea asked.

"Stinks."

"Hey, Brie!" Lea called out before telling Mary, "Hunter said you're invited to join us."

"No to whatever your weird boyfriend has planned. I want nothing to do with it."

Lea snorted in amusement. "We're just going to the zoo, silly."

"Exactly. What kind of lame-ass takes a grown woman to the zoo when they could be getting their freak on?"

"Whatever…"

"So, anyway, Stinks," Mary continued, dismissing Lea.

"Tell Brie she's invited to join us at the zoo with Hope if she wants," Lea called out.

"Ignore her," Mary advised Brie. "All they do is make out when they think no one is watching."

"We do not!" Lea protested.

"Yeah, right…"

"Anyhoo, let's get together soon, Brie," Lea sang out. "I miss my Stinky Cheese!"

"Get the hell out, Lea. I'm trying to have a conversation here."

"Fine, but my invitation still stands for you both."

Mary huffed loudly after the door closed. "Lea is a fucking pain to live with. Always cheerful and smiling, and those incessant jokes…it seriously makes me want to punch something."

Brie felt only sympathy for Mary. In her world of darkness and uncertainty, it was no wonder she found the happiness of others offensive to her.

"Is there anything I can do, Mary?"

"Just finish that fucking documentary about the dead violinist. I can take the heat as long as I know it's for a good cause."

"Oh, Mary…"

"Don't even start with me, bitch," she growled.

Brie frowned when she heard the dial tone. No one else in the world understood how incredibly selfless Mary was.

Mary Wilson was the strongest woman Brie had ever met, but her power was being crushed under the vile weight of Greg Holloway's malevolence.

Gifts of the Heart

Feeling a need to bring joy into someone's life, Brie went on a shopping spree for Autumn with her daughter Hope in tow.

She'd tried to call Autumn on several occasions, but each time, it went straight to voicemail. She wasn't sure if Autumn was ignoring all of calls or was simply too worried about Tono to deal with them.

Brie could only imagine how much her friend must be suffering, needing to remain strong for Tono without any outside support. Although Brie understood Tono's reason for keeping his health crisis a secret to protect Faelan, she still hated the thought of Autumn facing the uncertainty all alone.

Having experienced the benefit of the entire community's support when Sir was teetering on the edge of life or death, Brie knew how much it had helped. Without that support, she wasn't sure what would have happened to her—or Hope.

Although she couldn't fly to Korea herself to offer moral support, she wanted Autumn to know she was not alone. Remembering that terrible moment in her own life, Brie spent time thinking about her purchases for Autumn.

As soon as she arrived back home with her many packages, Brie began filling the large wicker basket with the plethora of comfort foods she'd purchased. She added a digital course on learning Japanese that Autumn could take with her wherever she went. Brie had found learning Italian a positive distraction when she had been at the hospital watching over Sir.

Brie also included a huge joke book full of terrible jokes, along with a fluffy blanket for those times when Autumn needed a warm hug. Hope had personally picked out the floppy stuffed bunny to go in the basket. Brie attached a tag to it and wrote, *Some bunny loves you.* She was certain Autumn would appreciate the silly humor.

Brie also threw in a couple of "gourmet" cans of soup in honor of Master Anderson, knowing how much his hot soup had warmed her soul on those days when she really needed it.

The last item she added to the basket was a picture frame with a photo of the three of them together. Lea stood in the center with her arms draped around Autumn and Brie. Engraved on the frame were the words, "Friends are like bras. Close to your heart and there for support."

Although Lea was in the dark about what was going on with Tono, Autumn needed to be reminded that Lea was still with her in spirit.

After carefully packing up the basket to be shipped across the world, Brie headed to the post office to have it overnighted. She was well-known at their post office because of her little PO box which was continually overflowing with letters from fans of the first documentary. It amazed Brie that they continued to reach out to her, wanting to express their love of the film and to share how it had changed their lives.

Brie was grateful for every letter, but today it left her feeling a little melancholy knowing the second film—which was even more powerful than the first—might never see the light of day.

"Oh, Mrs. Davis, let me help you with that," Polly called out when Brie walked up to the counter kicking the large box with her foot.

Polly ran through the counter's swinging gate and grabbed the heavy box off the floor for her.

"Thanks so much, Polly."

While Brie was paying her to ship it, Polly exclaimed, "Something just arrived for you from Italy. Let me get it for you!" She went into the back and returned holding a beautiful sapphire box.

"I wonder what it could be?" Brie asked in excitement, taking the box from her.

"I don't know, but it's got to be something special. We've never seen a shipping box this pretty before."

A smile spread across Brie's face when she saw the name of the company in gold print on the box—"Dante's Creazioni di Venezia".

Although it was pure torture, Brie chose to wait until she arrived home so she could open it with Sir. "Look what came all the way from Venice!" she said when she entered the house.

Sir raised an eyebrow when he read the address label.

"Interesting…"

"Isn't the box gorgeous? I almost hate to open it."

Brie was careful as she cut through the tape, and then laughed at herself when she saw there was an identical, but smaller, box inside which was wrapped in a silver bow. The attention to detail made unboxing Dante's gift a true experience.

She set the box on the desk and untied the ribbon. Lifting the lid, she set it to the side and sifted through the silver tissue paper.

Brie let out a gasp. Carefully picking it up, Brie gazed in sheer wonder at the jeweled Venetian mask. The delicate white mask was covered in sparkling crystals, and on the upper right side were amber stones in the shape of a violin. On the left were black jewels that made up five music notes. The pattern of notes on the staff was wavy like a flag fluttering in the wind, giving the musical notes a feeling of movement.

"Let me help you put it on, babygirl."

Brie held her breath as she laid the mask against her face and Sir secured the ties in the back. Once it was secure, he turned her around to look at it.

She saw Sir's eyes widen as he stared at the mask. "It is the most exquisite thing I have ever seen."

She smiled and hurried to the closest mirror to stare at her reflection. The genius of Dante's design was that the feminine shape complemented her face, but his intricate additions of the violin and musical notes enhanced the color of her eyes.

It was an extraordinary piece of art—one that belonged in a museum.

"I wonder what motivated him to create this?" Sir

asked, his voice full of admiration as he stared at the mask.

Brie laughed with embarrassment. "I actually asked him what he did for a living, not realizing he was a world-renowned mask designer. Dante explained the process to me, as well as his need for inspiration. I have to assume this design came to him after he watched Alonzo's first performance in America with me."

Sir untied the mask to examine it more closely. "There's something eerily familiar about it…" he muttered.

Brie tilted her head. "What do you mean, Sir?"

"These five notes. I feel as if I've heard this measure before, but I can't place the song." Sir handed Brie the mask and went to his music collection. After looking through it several times, he shook his head in frustration. "I thought my father played that song, but I have no recordings of it."

Brie frowned. "How strange."

"I suppose I must be mistaken." Sir laughed, but he stared at the mask, clearly intrigued by those five notes.

Brie picked up the box, certain Dante had left a note. She spied a small silver envelope tucked inside. She immediately opened it, hoping it held the answer.

Mrs. Davis,

In honor of Alonzo Davis and the conversation we shared at Signore Mancini's, I created this mask for you. It has been a long time since my muses have been so insistent. They completely consumed me.

It is my sincere hope that in the years to come,

you and Sir Davis enjoy the mask you inspired.

With gratitude,

Dante

"He says nothing about the music," Brie said as she handed the note to Sir.

He nodded while he read it. "My father had moments like Dante describes. When the music in his head had to find release and he'd spend days scribbling down the notes as they came to him."

Glancing at Brie, he smiled. "It was a wondrous thing to watch. I've never experienced it myself—can't really even comprehend it—but there was no doubt that other-worldly forces were involved whenever I watched my father during those times of inspiration."

Brie was fascinated by the revelation. "I never knew that, Sir."

He snorted. "Naturally, my mother didn't care for it."

"Why?"

"Papa ignored everything when it hit—including us. It was like he was possessed by the music playing in his head, and the only way to find release was by getting it down on paper. My father seemed completely consumed by it just like Dante describes."

"Didn't it bother you as a child?"

He shook his head, saying with pride in his voice, "It was part of him."

This was something Sir had never shared with her. After hearing about this part of Sir's childhood, Brie now had a deeper understanding of his father, Alonzo. He was not only a world-class violinist but an inspired composer.

Brie carefully placed the mask back in the box. "It wouldn't be proper for me to accept such an extravagant gift."

Sir surprised her when he said, "You must. This is an inspired piece. To return it would be a slap in the face for the artist who created it."

"But it must be worth hundreds."

He stared at the mask. "More like thousands, baby-girl."

Brie's jaw dropped. "Why would he give it away?"

Sir looked at her thoughtfully. "I remember my father telling me about a song he composed for someone he thought highly of—he never mentioned who. After spending weeks working on that one song, he finally felt it was ready and sent the music to them. Papa said he knew in his soul he had created a masterpiece."

Sir frowned when he added, "Several weeks later, he received it back in the mail. My father immediately tore up the music sheets and tossed them into the fireplace."

"Why would he do that?" Brie cried, mourning the loss of a song that would never be heard.

"Papa insisted it was created solely for that one person. Because it had been returned, he had no heart to play it."

Brie whimpered. "That's so sad…"

"I can't begin to understand, but I respect my father's feeling on the matter." He stared at the mask again. "This piece of art came from an other-worldly place and was meant specifically for you."

She picked up the mask feeling a sense of awe. "I'm

honored."

"As you should be, babygirl. To inspire a muse is a rare gift."

Sir stared at the notes on the mask again with a faint smile. "I must plan a grand scene worthy of this mask. For now, however, you must content yourself with the new instrument I have for you."

Her eyes widened. "What kind of instrument, Sir?"

He smiled seductively. "You'll find out tonight."

Brie let out an excited squeak. She always felt a special thrill experiencing something new with Sir.

She was unsure how she was going to concentrate on anything the rest of the day. It was one of the things she loved most about Sir. He knew how to draw out a scene, even before it began.

Brie shivered with delight, wondering what kinkiness he had in store for her.

By the time Brie put Hope to bed, she was already wet with anticipation. Sir had commanded she meet him in the bedroom once she was done. After closing Hope's door, she quickly headed downstairs.

Her heart was racing when she walked into the room and saw the open door to their secret playroom. Sir stood at the entrance, waiting for her.

The crimson walls of the room were covered in a multitude of instruments, which complemented the sexy wooden table with leather cuffs in the center of the room.

"Undress," he ordered in a sultry tone.

His simple command fanned the flames of her desire. With practiced grace, she unbuttoned her blouse, teasing him with sensual peeks of her naked skin before letting the blouse fall to the floor. Rather than feeling self-conscious of her round belly, Brie was extremely proud of it because it represented the potency of their love.

She playfully shimmied out of her skirt next, then turned away from Sir to undo her bra. Glancing over her shoulder with a seductive gaze, she held it out before dropping it onto her pile of clothing. Brie slowly turned around for him so he could admire her.

Sir stared lustfully at her ample breasts and motioned her to him. "I'll take care of those panties."

She glided to him and felt a thrill as he pulled out the knife he used for wax play from his pocket. With two quick movements, her panties lay in tatters on the floor. Sliding his hand between her legs, he nodded his approval.

"Already wet for me."

"Yes, Master. I have ached for you all day."

His eyes flashed wickedly. "I long to see how you react tonight."

Brie glanced at his wall of tools, curious if he had already added it to his collection, but she saw nothing new.

Sir followed her gaze and chuckled lightly. "What you seek is in my suit pocket."

Brie turned her attention back on him, surprised that the instrument would be so small.

Sir slowly reached into his jacket but kept his hand

closed when he pulled it out.

"Curious?" he asked, holding out his fist.

She nodded enthusiastically.

The glint in his eye suddenly made her nervous. He slowly opened his hand to reveal a cute tweezer clamp with purple tips and a tiny silver heart hanging off the end of it. It reminded her of nipple clamps, except there was only one of them.

She giggled and looked up at Sir. "I don't understand."

"This is a clitoral clamp."

Brie's pussy clenched. Although she enjoyed the playful pain of nipple clamps, she had never considered what torturing her sensitive clit would feel like.

"I can tell by your expression, the idea of it makes you uncomfortable," he stated in a smooth, seductive voice.

"I love my clit, Sir."

He chuckled. "I love your clit, too."

"Will it hurt?"

Sir answered with a sexy smirk. "There's only one way to find out. But first, we must stimulate that shy little clit."

He suddenly swept her up in his arms and carried her to the table. Positioning her ass close to the edge, he began binding her right ankle.

Brie let out a nervous sigh, excited that he was challenging her in this new way, but uncertain whether she would enjoy the experience.

"You always have your safeword, babygirl," he reminded her as he spread her legs and bound her left ankle—leaving her completely helpless and open to him.

Sir took off his jacket, slipping the clamp into his breast pocket before attending to his sleeves. Brie found it such a turn-on to watch the meticulous way he rolled up his sleeves before a scene. It was enough to make a girl dripping wet.

Once he was done, Sir gazed down at her. "I notice you're breathing faster."

Brie nodded, smiling up at him. There was no point in denying it.

Sir left her for a moment to grab a tool off one of the shelves. Brie grinned when he turned around and she saw his instrument of choice. She *loved* the Magic Wand. Its intense vibration made for the most delicious orgasms in no time at all.

When Sir turned it on, her body instantly responded like Pavlov's dog. The sound of the loud buzzing made her pussy even wetter as she anticipated the powerful orgasm which was soon to follow.

He pressed it against the right side of her clit, and then slowly rolled it over to the other side. Her entire pussy vibrated from the large head of the wand, making her shiver in delight.

It only took a couple of seconds before she felt the stirrings of her first climax beginning to build. Just before she reached the crest, Sir pulled the instrument away.

"That should do it."

Brie whimpered.

Sir chuckled as he swirled his finger over her swollen clit, causing her moan in pleasure.

"Now that your clit is erect, I can easily attach the clamp."

She glanced nervously at the innocent-looking thing when he pulled it out of his breast pocket.

There it was all cute and delicate looking. But, after years of experience, Brie knew that you could never judge the intensity of an instrument simply by its looks.

"Are you ready, téa?"

Brie nodded, swallowing anxiously.

"I want your verbal consent."

She sucked in her breath, letting it out slowly before she answered, "Yes, Master. I am ready."

He leaned down between her legs and slipped the clamp over both sides of her clit. Pressing the tweezer clamp together, he slowly adjusted the ring to increase the pressure.

Brie was nervous about that type of constriction and whimpered.

"Color, téa?"

"I don't know."

"Does it hurt?" he asked.

She concentrated on the feeling itself, rather than her fear of it. "No, Master. It feels strange."

"I'm going to tighten it a little more."

She held her breath as he increased the pressure slightly.

"Color, téa?"

"Green, Master."

"That should do well for now."

As she lay there, she found the clamp created a fiery ache and she enjoyed the sensation.

Sir observed quietly for several moments before asking, "Color?"

"Very green," she answered with excitement.

"I thought you'd like it," Sir replied with his chocolaty smooth voice.

Brie stared up at the mirrored ceiling above her with a silly grin on her face. Who knew a clitoral clamp could actually feel good?

Now that Sir was satisfied with the tension of the clamp, he slipped two fingers into her pussy and began slowly stimulating her G-spot. Since he had already used the Magic Wand, her pussy was primed for a climax.

"Am I allowed to come, Master?"

"Not yet," he answered with amusement.

Brie bit her lip.

As Sir continued to play with her G-spot, he repositioned himself so he could kiss her on the lips. Brie returned his kiss with all the pent-up desire he'd created earlier after telling her about tonight's adventure.

The boosted blood flow to her clit caused by the toy made her pussy tingle without it even being touched. When Sir's hand brushed against her clit as he penetrated her with his fingers, she experienced a burst of intense sensation.

She moaned into Sir's mouth, completely overwhelmed by the feel of it. "More…" she begged.

"I can only leave this on for ten minutes."

She pouted.

He tsked gently. "We don't want to do any damage to this beautiful clit no matter how good it feels, now do we?"

Brie shook her head.

He stared at her intently as he continued to play with her, building up the tension of her impending climax. When it finally became too much, she cried out even though she was enjoying his exquisite torture.

Thrashing her head back and forth, she moaned loudly as her pussy throbbed with every beat of her heart. She'd thought the Magic Wand was challenging, but this stimulation was equally so—but in a completely different way.

Sir bit her lower lip before pulling away from their kiss. He stared at her hungrily as he licked his fingers. "I'm still addicted to the taste of Brie."

The man was pure primal masculinity!

"Time's up," he announced as he moved between her legs to remove the clamp. He looked over her bulging stomach and smiled. "Now, for the real fun."

Brie breathed sharply in and out. She had no idea what he meant but trusted him completely as he took off the clamp. A squeak escaped her lips when the blood flooded back in.

The tingling sensation the clamp had caused increased tenfold and felt incredible!

That's when Sir settled between her legs and she felt his first long lick…

Oh, my God!

The softness of his tongue mixed with the heightened sensitivity from the clamp was out of this world. She never thought such a thing was possible.

When Sir chuckled, she could feel the low vibrations of his lips against her pussy, driving her even wilder.

"Yes, téa. You now have my permission to come."

Brie cried out as she gave in to the incredible sensations. The orgasm that rocketed through her body not only stole her breath away, but all intelligent thought. Caught up in a wave of ecstasy, she felt tears of erotic bliss roll down her cheeks. She rode the crest of each wave that followed, giving in to the magic he had created.

When it finally ended, she let out a shuddering breath. Her thighs were still quivering from the power of it.

Sir looked up from between her legs.

"Color, téa?"

Brie made a sound, but she had no idea what came out.

He smiled knowingly and returned to her pussy. Brie stared up at the ceiling, completely enraptured by her reflection.

There she was, naked on the table, with her long curls framing her face, her breasts full and inviting, her belly round and beautiful, and the sexiest man alive between her legs as he went down on her with gusto.

Brie felt like she had died and gone to erotic heaven...

Welcomed Distraction

Several days later, Rytsar called with an update for them. "Before you ask, *radost moya*, I am fine."

Brie laughed and then opened her mouth to ask her next question, but he was quick to answer that too. "Yes, the Wallace boy is doing as well as can be expected. It seems the cold weather agrees with the wolf in him."

"What about Lilly?"

Rytsar's low groan made the hairs rise on the back of her neck.

"Is there a problem?" Sir asked with concern.

"With her, always, *moy droog*."

"Do you need me to come?"

"*Nyet*. You would only complicate things."

"How so?"

Rytsar cleared his throat. "Do you remember the issue the Reverend Mother was having with her?"

Sir gave Brie a troubled glance before answering, "Yes."

"Apparently, she's become so obsessed that they've had to lock her in her room. The creature must be supervised by two people at all times whenever she is released."

Brie gasped. "What happened?"

"I am ashamed to say, *radost moya*."

Sir squeezed Brie's hand in reassurance, telling Rytsar, "It is important we know."

Rytsar hesitated for a moment before granting his request. "She has continually cornered the Reverend Mother when she finds her alone and begs her to…" His voice trailed away.

"Go on," Sir insisted.

"To penetrate her with a stick."

"Dear God." Sir closed his eyes, shaking his head.

"It's gotten to the point where the Reverend Mother fears for the creature's safety."

Brie was confused. "Why was she afraid for Lilly?"

Rytsar let out a disgusted sigh. "When the Reverend Mother refused to do the act, Lilly attempted to do it herself while the venerable woman was watching."

"Oh, hell," Sir said with revulsion. "The poor Reverend Mother."

Brie felt physically ill. She could only imagine how horrifying it must be for the godly woman to be confronted with that. But it also upset Brie to know Lilly was *that* unhinged.

"It is unfortunate that I cannot take the creature off her hands immediately. However, the Reverend Mother and I agree securing the best facility is crucial and she is willing to wait it out."

"I should have anticipated it would only get worse," Sir muttered.

"One good thing has come of it."

"What's that?" Brie asked, needing to hear something hopeful.

"The effect it has had on the Wolf Pup. After hearing the Mother Reverend's story and seeing Lilly for himself, he is as driven as I am to extinguish the threat."

"We're just talking about finding a suitable facility, right?" Brie pressed.

"Naturally, *radost moya.* I will do nothing against the creature until you give the word."

Brie shivered, noting he'd said *until* rather than *if.* She sincerely hoped that day would never come.

"So, would you say Wallace is improving?" Sir asked him.

"I wouldn't go that far," Rytsar answered bluntly. "However, this situation has given him something to focus on, which is crucial right now. The boy needs time to process through the loss. In his current state, time is not his friend—but it will be."

"So, Faelan's not any better?" Brie whimpered.

"Not yet, *radost moya.* It will take time. However, there is a fire in his eye when he talks about the creature. It is not only you and Hope he is concerned about protecting, but his own child. His wish to help will serve well enough for now."

Brie was relieved to hear there was still fight left in Faelan, but the world was a truly twisted place when Lilly could inspire something positive.

"Now that you've had time to assess the situation, how long do you think it will take to build the facility?" Sir asked.

"Honestly, *moy droog,* I don't foresee any of this going quickly."

Brie could hear the defeat in Sir's voice. "I'm afraid I agree. But I am sorry, old friend."

Rytsar laughed. "For what? I have the power to build an environment that is guaranteed to eliminate the threat. That is priceless to me. As far as Wallace, I welcome the challenge he presents."

Sir's voice was tinged with regret. "I have had to lean on you too many times in the last few years."

Rytsar's tone became deadly serious. "*Moy droog*, you and I both have jobs to do. You must take care of *radost moya* until the birth of the child, and I must deal with this creature."

"My problems should not be placed on your shoulders."

"We are brothers," the Russian replied passionately. "That is the way of family."

"I…" Sir suddenly choked up and had to clear his throat. "I don't know how to repay you for everything you have done, Anton."

"You forget what you sacrificed for me when we were younger—but a Durov never forgets."

"Like an elephant," Brie interjected, wanting to bring levity to the difficult conversation.

"*Da*, but more like a prehistoric mammoth with massive tusks that will rip apart all of its enemies."

Sir smiled slightly, nodding to Brie.

"Is there any chance we could speak to Faelan?" she asked, needing to hear his voice.

"I would put him on the phone, but he is still licking his wounds and is not up for the task."

Brie frowned. "Can you let him know we are thinking of him, and Grace is being well cared for?"

"I will," he assured her.

"Durov, give me something I can do to help, damn it," Sir demanded.

Rytsar thought for a moment. "There is something, *moy droog*…"

"Name it."

"I have a craving for a particular donut. *Radost moya* knows the one."

Brie smiled, remembering when Rytsar had shared his secret obsession with her. "I've never forgotten those donuts."

"Better send one for the Pup, as well. It would be unfair not to share, but I don't like sharing—with *anyone*," Rytsar added with an ominous growl.

She giggled, recalling how upset he'd gotten with her when she'd snuck a bite of his Blueberry Bourbon donut.

"I will see to it, but I would like to do more," Sir replied.

"Fine. There is something else you can do. Enjoy this time with your wife and unborn child. You were denied that chance with Hope, so make the most of it now, *moy droog*."

"Brother…"

"Knowing you are both happy sustains me," Rytsar stated. "I promise to call if anything changes."

"Call even if nothing changes," Brie begged.

Rytsar chuckled. "Fine, just to keep you from worrying because it is not good for the growing babe."

Brie rubbed her stomach. She realized Rytsar might not be back in time for the birth, and the thought made her extremely sad. "I hope things go better than you expect, and you come back soon."

"What will be, will be, *radost moya*," he answered somberly. "I cannot leave until the creature is locked away and Wallace is strong enough for the challenges he must face."

"We are grateful to you," Sir replied, his voice gruff with emotion.

Brie could almost hear the smirk in Rytsar's voice when he answered, "Do not concern yourself, *moy droog*. I am a man with multiple talents."

Before he hung up, Rytsar told Brie, "Do me a favor, *radost moya*."

"Of course."

"I am sending you a recording. Play it for *moye solntse* and the new babe."

Tears filled Brie's eyes, touched by his request. "It would be my honor, Rytsar."

With each passing day, Brie found herself growing increasingly anxious, and it frightened her. "Sir, I think something is seriously wrong, but I don't know what."

Taking her fear seriously, Sir had her sit down so they could talk about it. "What's foremost on your mind right now?"

She rubbed her stomach. "I keep trying to convince myself the delivery will be fine, but after Hope's difficult birth and knowing what happened to Kylie…" She looked him in the eyes, her heart racing. "I'm scared, Sir."

"That's a completely reasonable reaction. I'm sure,

like me, you have done plenty of research and found that what happened with Kylie is rare and there is no reason to suspect it will happen to you."

It brought Brie comfort to know Sir had been concerned enough to research the issue himself.

"What else is bothering you?"

"I can't help worrying about Faelan and the effect his absence might be having on his baby."

Sir nodded, a thoughtful look on his face. "We have to trust Durov can guide Wallace through the loss of Kylie. As far as the child is concerned, I have been checking in with Celestia. As you know, they have been overwhelmed by the generosity of the community. The last time we spoke, Celestia told me Grace is crying less often and smiling more. I think you can set those concerns aside for now."

Brie smiled, grateful to hear the baby was doing better.

"Is there anything else?" Sir asked, looking at her intently.

Although she was deeply concerned about Mary's toxic relationship with Holloway, she kept her promise not to share what was happening with Sir. Instead, she brought up her lingering disappointment about the film director, Finn, turning his back on her.

"I understand his actions left you feeling disillusioned, babygirl. But it's better to know now who your friends are. As unsavory as this experience with Holloway has been, he inadvertently helped you by revealing who you can trust in the film industry."

"Sir, that's just it. I can't trust anyone."

He corrected her. "Mary has had your back the entire

time. Put your trust in the people who would never betray you. One true comrade is worth a thousand wannabes."

Brie nodded, his words cementing her decision not to break her vow with Mary. She sincerely hoped Sir would understand when the truth eventually came out.

"Is there anything else, babygirl?"

Brie let out a nervous sigh. "Lilly."

He frowned, his eyes flashing with a mix of anger and concern.

"Even though Rytsar is securing a new facility, I still worry about her, Sir. I don't know if I will ever stop being terrified of Lilly."

Sir sighed heavily. "Until that creature draws her last breath, she will remain a threat to us. However, you and I made a choice we can both live with. You understand the alternative, so you must hold onto the reasons behind that decision whenever fear threatens to over-whelm you."

"I'll try, Sir."

He raised an eyebrow.

"I mean, I *will*, Sir," Brie amended, deeply grateful for his understanding and insight.

Sir looked at her thoughtfully. "Baron keeps inquir-ing about you. Would you be up for a visit tomorrow?"

Brie smiled when she heard Baron's name. "I would love that, Sir. It's been a long time since we've seen him."

He nodded. "I agree. Are you still interested in doing a lesson together before the birth? It might prove a welcome distraction."

She looked at her large belly and laughed. "Do you

really think he would want my help in this state?"

"It wouldn't be an issue unless you're uncomfortable with it."

She gazed into Sir's eyes and realized that he needed the distraction as well. Being able to give him the gift of teaching again, even if it was only for one session, would make her profoundly happy.

"I would love to, Sir."

He leaned down and kissed her tenderly. "Then I will let Baron know."

Baron insisted they bring Hope with them because he hadn't seen her for months. As soon as he opened the door and saw their little girl, he shook his head in disbelief. "There's nothing like children to show how quickly time passes."

Baron then glanced at Brie's stomach and grinned.

With a nod from Sir, Baron gave Brie a long, warm hug. "It has been far too long, kitten," he said in his low, velvety voice.

"It sure has," she agreed, squeezing him tight.

Brie felt a deep sense of gratitude to Baron. He was the Dom who first introduced her to the fun of a jeweled butt plug. He'd been so tender and gentle during her first session that she had never forgotten it. Baron had also helped her overcome the abuse from her past with Darius.

Baron was her hero in the true sense of the word because he'd saved her when she had been drugged by a predator posing as a Dom while visiting the Kinky Goat years ago with Lea and Mary. His need to protect defenseless subs was something she sincerely admired and would be forever grateful for.

"How have you been?" she asked, smiling up at him.

His hazel eyes sparkled as a grin spread across his face. "Working hard and enjoying every minute of it."

"So, your classes are going well?"

"We're thriving—which is both good and bad."

Brie furrowed her brow in surprise. "How so?"

"Word spread fast about what we are doing here. It crushes me whenever I have to tell a desperate sub there is a long waiting list."

"Have you thought of expanding?" Sir asked him.

Baron shook his head. "Captain, Candy, and I have spoken extensively about it. We feel good about the program we have now, but we are at full capacity as it is. We cannot expand without compromising the curriculum, since each sub we work with needs extensive care and individual attention.

"What the three of you are doing is truly beautiful," Brie told him, bursting with gratitude as she hugged Hope against her.

Baron's smile widened. "It is the most fulfilling thing I have ever done. I know Adrianna would be proud of our efforts."

Sir clasped his shoulder. "Of that, I have no doubt."

Brie looked at Baron tenderly, knowing how much he still cared for the submissive he'd lost years ago.

"So, tell me. What's kept you two so busy, besides the obvious," Baron asked with a knowing wink.

Only a select few in their circle knew the hell they'd

suffered because of Lilly, or Brie's failed offer with her documentary. So, Brie told him, "I've been busy researching my next documentary about Alonzo Davis."

"Is that going well?"

"It's been exciting," she gushed. "I love learning about the man behind the talent."

"And you, Sir Davis?" Baron asked, turning to him.

"Work never seems to end," Sir replied, unable to divulge more.

"I'm curious—do you miss your training days at the Center?"

Sir let out a low chuckle. "Actually, it's one of the reasons we came tonight."

Baron's eyes lit up. "I was hoping you'd say that."

"While we don't have much time before the birth, we would like to be involved with your program."

Baron looked at both of them excitedly. "You can't know what this will mean to our subs. To see a healthy D/s couple building a family together would be inspiring and comforting to them."

He looked at Brie, his voice tinged with sorrow. "So many of our student have been deeply scarred and no longer believe such a future exists for them."

Her heart hurt for all the submissives who had been abused by predators posing as Doms. She couldn't begin to imagine the trauma they'd experienced and truly hoped she could bring comfort to them in some meaningful way.

"Would you like to come with me to see The Power Exchange?"

"Is that what you call your dungeon?" Brie asked, charmed by the name.

"Yes, we find our students react negatively to the word 'dungeon' due to past experiences."

"How many have graduated from the course?" Sir asked him as they walked down the stairs to Baron's secret room.

"Twenty-two, so far," he stated proudly. "We never force anyone to leave until they are ready. Eleven have moved on to healthy D/s relationships, while the majority are active in the community again. Two of our subs have chosen to pursue vanilla relationships. We consider each a win."

"Considering the maltreatment they've had to overcome, it's truly remarkable," Sir said with admiration.

"Like the Training Center, once a student, always a student. Any of our graduates can contact us if issues arise. It's another reason we chose not to expand."

Knowing how important Lea and Mary were to her during and after her training, Brie understood the importance of what they were doing. "It's like you are creating a big family for the submissives who attend here."

"Yes, we want them to feel that way. They understand each other and can support one another better than anyone else. Our main goal is to establish the acceptable standards they should expect from their Dominants, and help guide them to a point where they can trust again."

"Not an easy task," Sir stated.

"No, it requires patience and time, but the reward is seeing their confidence blossom." Baron smiled again. "It's a unique high I never tire of."

They walked down an enchanting circular staircase.

When Brie entered the room, she gasped in delight. Baron had described the room to her once, but words could not do justice to the far wall covered in a mosaic of erotic scenes of Rome. It was breathtaking and brought an element of elegance to the chamber that no other dungeon had.

Brie glanced around at the antique St. Andrew's Cross, the whipping poles with gold chains, sumptuously padded spanking benches, intricately carved wooden stockades, and the decorative cages. Every piece of equipment matched the opulence of the mosaic.

"Wow, this place looks so inviting!"

Baron nodded. "That was Candy's doing. She wants it to feel welcoming to each submissive who walks into The Power Exchange."

Sir scanned the large area. "I see there are no private areas for play."

"It was strategic on our part. Knowing our students suffer from trust issues, we want the place where they scene to be completely open. That way, there's no need for them to fear what might be happening behind closed doors."

"A prudent decision," Sir stated.

Brie nodded her agreement. "That would be extremely important to the submissives."

Sir asked, "What kind of demonstration do you feel would benefit your students at this point?"

"The thing you are famous for, Sir Davis. The importance of touch in the D/s dynamic."

Brie grinned, happy her pregnancy would in no way impact such a lesson.

Glancing at Brie, Baron added, "One of our current

submissives is three months along, so it will be an empowering lesson for her to observe how D/s can work in all stages of pregnancy."

"That is an excellent suggestion, Baron," Sir stated. "Is there a separate area for discussions?"

"No, we do everything right here, Sir Davis. However, we start each class upstairs in the kitchen."

"Really?" Brie suddenly remembering her humiliating attempts at omelets when she was going through her own submissive training at the Center.

"We firmly believe that beginning each session with an informal gathering to share snacks and talk about their day helps break down the walls they have built up."

Baron turned to Sir. "We want our students to relate to us outside the formal dynamic of teacher/student, so they form a higher level of trust."

"You have truly created a unique program here," Sir complimented.

"Candy's experience with abuse has helped us hone in on what is important to our students."

"I hate that Candy ever experienced it," Brie replied, thinking back on the day she'd handed Candy the business card to the Training Center. Brie had never forgotten the haunted look in Candy's eyes while her repulsive wannabe Dom loomed over her. "It's inspiring that she has been able to create something beautiful out of such a terrible experience."

"I couldn't agree more," Baron said. "I'm proud to work by her side."

Brie was deeply touched by the difference her friends were making. It was both humbling and exciting to be asked to be part of their endeavor.

She glanced at Sir, and her heart skipped a beat. She hadn't seen that look in his eyes since he was Headmaster of the Training Center.

"How long should the session be?" Sir asked him.

"We normally do short sessions, with an extensive discussion afterward. However, you are free to take as long as you want."

"I think an hour would suffice."

"Perfect, Sir Davis. I'm certain our students will have plenty to ask you." He glanced at Brie. "Both of you."

Sir put his arm around her. "We welcome all questions they might have."

Brie suddenly felt butterflies in her stomach. Although it was only one session, seeing the excitement in Sir's eyes thrilled her beyond words.

Ever since he collared her and walked away from the Training Center, she had dreamed of this day...

His Calling

B rie's mom drove over to pick up Hope so they would have time to prepare for the lesson.

Brie had shared her excitement about this rare opportunity with her mom, who understood how important it was to her. But, knowing her husband's opinion about their lifestyle, her mother had chosen not to share any details with her dad.

Brie secretly wished her father could accept her lifestyle, but she pacified herself with the fact that he respected Thane enough not to argue about it anymore.

However, if Brie was truly honest with herself, it hurt that she couldn't share exciting things like this with her dad. The "don't ask, don't tell" stance he enforced made her feel as if she should be ashamed of it.

Oh, if her dad could fully accept her for who she was, it would mean everything to her. But at least her mother accepted her unique relationship with Sir and wanted to support Brie in any way she could.

Brie grabbed the diaper bag and handed it to her. "Thanks again, Mom. You have no idea what a relief it is to know Hope has a loving place to go to whenever we need it."

Her mother's light laughter filled the air. "You have no idea how much we look forward to her visits."

Turning to Sir, her mother took Hope from his arms. "You'll understand the thrill when you have grandchildren of your own."

Sir chuckled. "That's a long way off."

"I know," she giggled. "I just want you to know that things get even sweeter with time."

He looked at her thoughtfully. "I never believed that was possible before Brie. The reminder is appreciated."

Her mom beamed up at him. "You make such a great father, Thane. I look forward to seeing what kind of grandfather you'll be."

Brie stared at Sir, imagining him with salt and pepper hair.

Oh, God, he's going to look even more handsome…

She blushed when her mom caught her staring at Sir. Hopefully, she had no idea that the thought of an older version of Sir was making Brie's panties wet.

"Don't you worry about a thing, you two. Go and enjoy teaching your classes together."

"It's only a single session," Sir amended, "but we will. Thank you."

"Who knows? I'm sure you'll do an excellent job and they'll insist you come back."

Sir glanced at Brie when he told her, "While that would be an honor, Brie's health is my main concern right now."

Marcy grinned at her daughter. "Hard to believe I'll be meeting my next grandchild soon and I don't even know if it's a boy or a girl."

"I like that it's a mystery," Brie confessed to her.

"Truth is—I don't care either way, sweetheart. I'm just glad I get to be here for the birth!"

Knowing her mom would be there brought Brie enormous peace of mind and she hugged her tight. "You being here means so much to me, Mom."

When Brie broke the hug, her mother cradled her face in her hands. "I'm the luckiest mother alive. I have a talented daughter who found the perfect man to make her happy."

Brie smiled at Sir. "I'm the lucky one."

"And just look at the beautiful cherub you two created together," her mother cooed, bouncing Hope in her arms.

"She is a little angel," Sir agreed, gazing at his daughter.

"So, I'm off! I'll see you two tomorrow before noon."

"Would you rather we swing by to get her?" Sir offered.

"No, I want you two to bask in your success after your class."

Brie's mom knew exactly how they would be celebrating that success. The fact she was arranging a time for them to be alone was an extremely thoughtful gift.

Soon after she left, Sir grabbed the keys to his Lotus and held out his hand to her. "Come with me, Brie."

Her heart fluttered, remembering when he had said those exact words to her the night of the collaring.

Sir was skillful behind the wheel, driving his sports car like he dominated a sub—pushing the limits of the vehicle with precision. Brie flushed with excitement as he cut sharp corners, then hit the gas when they got on the freeway.

The rush she felt was close to orgasmic! Her heart was still racing when they reached Baron's home. "That was fun!"

Sir winked at her before getting out of the car. He walked around and opened the passenger door to help her out of the low-lying vehicle. It was not a graceful task at her stage of pregnancy, which made her giggle as she got out of the car.

As he escorted Brie to the door, Sir asked, "How are you feeling about tonight?"

She let out an excited squeak. "I can't wait, Sir! It's like taking our scene to a whole new level, knowing it might help some of the subs here."

He nodded, his eyes flashing with excitement. "I agree. It does add a unique element to the exchange."

Brie's heart fluttered when she saw the glint in his eyes.

Candy answered the door with a wide smile. Bowing her head respectfully, she addressed Sir first. "Please come in, Sir Davis."

Then she grabbed Brie's hand enthusiastically, pulling her inside. "I can't tell you how thrilled I am about tonight! Our subs are so anxious to meet you."

Captain joined them, wearing a stylish eyepatch and looking younger than Brie had ever seen him. "This has been a long time coming, Sir Davis." He held out his hand.

Sir shook it, adding somberly, "Yes. We spoke about it the day the plane crashed."

A chill traveled down Brie's spine when Sir mentioned the accident. It made tonight's session an even bigger accomplishment, considering how hard he'd had to fight to come back after that tragic day.

"Are you ready to teach again?"

Sir smirked at Captain. "I have been—even before that fateful day."

Captain's blue eye flickered with understanding. "I'm glad to hear it. Please follow me."

Brie held her breath as she walked beside Candy, listening to the excited chatter of the subs in the next room as they made their way down the hallway. The group sounded so relaxed, like a group of women and men chatting at an informal gathering.

As soon as Captain walked into the room, however, everyone became silent. "Students, I would like to introduce you to Sir Davis, former Headmaster of the Submissive Training Center and his submissive, Brianna Davis, one of the top graduates of the program."

The subs all bowed their heads, the casual feeling in the room suddenly becoming more reserved and strained.

Sir chuckled lightly. "No need for formalities. We're here as a D/s couple tonight, nothing more."

A few of the subs looked up and then smiled when they saw him grab a paper plate and start filling it with the snacks laid out on the counter. He commanded Brie to sit and placed the plate beside her.

She smiled up at him, picking up a cracker from the plate. "Thank you, Sir."

One of the male subs joined them and asked hesitantly, "Can I ask you a question, Sir Davis?"

"You may, but I reserve the right not to answer," he replied with a slight smile.

"I don't mean any disrespect, but do other Doms make fun of you for serving your sub like that?"

"It's only natural that I, as her Dominant, would want to take care of my sub and the child she carries."

The sub nodded thoughtfully.

"Any Dom worth his salt is concerned about his sub's well-being as much as he is his own—if not more so," he answered in a casual tone as he filled his own plate. "A Dom who would question my motives is highlighting their lack of understanding of what it means to be a Dominant."

Baron walked up and asked Sir, "How was the traffic?"

"Not bad." Glancing at Brie he added with a smirk. "In fact, the drive was quite exhilarating."

Brie nodded enthusiastically.

As they continued to talk, the casual chatter from before returned. Brie stared at Sir, admiring how easily he had diffused the stiffness that had overtaken the room.

He understood the needs of these students and had quickly taken the measures necessary to meet them.

A young woman sat beside Brie as she took nibbles from her plate. "How far along are you, may I ask?"

"I'm heading into the home stretch. Five more weeks to go," Brie told her proudly.

"Wow!" The girl rubbed her own stomach. "I'm only three months along."

"Congratulations!"

She smiled hesitantly. After several moments, she

confessed, "My Dom left me after he found out." Tears suddenly welled up in the girl's eyes. "He punished me severely for lying when I told him it was his."

Brie was overcome with sympathy for the young woman. "I'm so sorry."

The girl shrugged. "I guess I get to be a single mom—never wanted to be."

"That's a huge responsibility, but there is also great joy in being a mother."

The girl offered her a cautious smile.

Brie put her food down and held out her hand. "I'm Brie. What's your name?"

"Lily."

Surprised to hear the name, Brie forced herself not to flinch because she didn't want to upset the innocent girl.

"A lovely name," Sir stated, placing a reassuring hand on Brie's shoulder.

"Thank you, Sir Davis," Lily replied shyly, a blush rising to her cheeks.

Sir had that effect on submissives. His natural dominance called to them, and they subconsciously reacted to it.

"Lily was just telling me she's three months pregnant, Sir."

His eyes softened. "I hope you are feeling well."

"I am...now."

"Let us know if there is anything we can do to help in the months ahead." He glanced at Brie and smiled at her warmly.

Sir's obvious concern for Lily's welfare seemed to boost the girl's confidence, and she blushed an even deeper shade of pink. "Thank you, Sir Davis."

Brie gazed at Sir with gratitude. He had never lost his ability to read people and respond in a way that empowered them. That talent was an incredible asset in an environment like tonight.

Baron rejoined them and asked Sir, "Will you need time to set up?"

He shook his head. "No, tonight's session is all about this…" He held up his hands. "No prep necessary."

Brie felt the butterflies start again.

Baron slapped him on the back. "Fine, then we will start the session in five minutes."

Turning to the group of five women and two men, Baron said, "This is your five-minute warning."

The chatter increased as the subs finished their plates and quickly cleaned up. Brie glanced at Candy, who was grinning amid the chaos, looking every bit like a proud mom as she helped them.

Captain joined Sir. "Let me take you downstairs."

Lily took Brie's plate and smiled shyly at Sir as she walked away.

Placing his hand on the small of Brie's back, Sir followed Captain downstairs.

The large room had been transformed for the session. There was now a row of folding chairs placed in a semicircle in the center of the room.

"What furniture will you need tonight?" Captain asked.

"A sturdy chair will suffice."

Although Captain was an older gentleman, he easily picked up a large wooden chair in the corner.

"Let me help you with that," Sir offered.

"No need," Captain assured him. Brie watched with admiration as the muscled sixty-year-old placed it in front of the row of folding chairs. "Will this do?"

"Perfect," Sir stated.

Minutes later, Brie heard the group heading downstairs to meet them. For some unknown reason, she suddenly felt nervous.

However, these weren't the kind of nerves that she had when she was worried something might go wrong.

No! It was more like euphoria—a feeling of everything finally coming together after years of dreaming of this.

"Are you ready, téa?"

She grinned at Sir. "I have never been more ready, Master."

He chuckled softly, wrapping an arm around her as the students filed in and sat down. Captain, Candy, and Baron sat in the chairs that had been placed to the side. It was less formal than the long table the trainers used at the Center, but it still allowed the three to observe their students during the session.

Brie was impressed by how much care had been put into their unique curriculum. She knew they wanted to ensure their students felt safe and comfortable at every point of their class.

Once everyone was settled, Baron stood up. "As you know, Sir Davis and Brianna have come tonight to introduce you to the power of touch during a scene. Without further ado, I'll hand over the reins to Sir Davis." He nodded to Sir before sitting down.

Everyone was silent as the feeling of expectation rose in the room.

Sir turned to address the students. "I suspect for many of you, the touch of the person you gave your power over to has not always been a positive experience. It should be in all circumstances—even in punishment."

Someone in the group let out an audible gasp, obviously surprised by Sir's statement.

Another submissive immediately raised his hand.

Sir called on him. "Yes?"

"How is that possible? Punishment is meant to hurt."

"True. It is used for correction. However, the difference is the spirit in which it is given. That is something my submissive and I will be demonstrating tonight."

The submissive nodded his head slowly, obviously still confused by Sir's assertion.

"Before I begin, I would like to introduce you to my submissive." He held out his hand for Brie to join him. "Brianna has been my sub for over three and a half years. In that time, we married and as you can see, we are expecting our second child."

Another hand shot up.

Captain immediately addressed the group. "It would be best to leave your questions until the end of the session."

Sir gave the sub an easy smile. "Normally, I do not invite questions until the end of the scene. However, tonight, if any of you have burning questions that cannot wait, I will answer it."

He turned his attention to the sub who'd raised her hand. "What is your question?"

"Why did you get married? Isn't a collar enough?"

Sir glanced at Brie. "It was a personal decision based

on Brie's desire to be wed and my desire for the world to acknowledge our union legally. Was it necessary? No. However, it was the right decision for us. BDSM is a personal journey that is defined by the individual partners involved."

"Thank you for that answer, Sir Davis," the woman replied, bowing her head.

Addressing the group, Sir stated, "Normally, a spanking bench would be used for this demonstration, but the physical constraints of pregnancy required a modification."

Turning to Brie, Sir commanded, "Strip down to your underwear, téa."

Her heart sped up as she slowly removed her clothes in front of her Master. Her focus was now entirely on him—no one else in the room mattered.

Sir had requested Brie dress in the sexy but comfortable uniform he had given her for their sessions at the Submissive Training Center. She was grateful for it as she gracefully kicked off her low strapless heels. Using the chair for balance, she slipped off her skirt next. The entire time, she kept glancing at Sir seductively, inviting his gaze.

Brie felt no shame in exposing her pregnant body to everyone in the room and she knew it had everything to do with Sir's expression as he watched her undress. The pride in his eyes as she removed each piece of clothing and exposed her naked skin to him made her blush with pleasure.

When she was done, Sir commanded, "Kneel on the seat, facing the back of the chair, and use it for support."

Brie mounted the heavy chair, her knees resting on

the seat as she held onto the back of the chair, leaning her torso against it. The coolness of the basement and her own excitement caused her nipples to harden.

Sir grazed his hand lightly over her skin. The instant he made contact, she felt a bolt of electricity course through her and moaned softly.

"It is possible to have an entire scene that only utilizes the power of touch. First, I stimulate the skin with light touches to fan her level of desire."

Brie closed her eyes, a smile on her lips as his hand passed over her ass and traveled down her thigh.

"To increase her sensitivity to my touch, I enjoy blindfolding her. Blindfolds are something my submissive responds to well, but it may be a trigger for some of you and is unnecessary for the scene."

Brie's heart rate increased when she felt the material of the blindfold covering her eyes as he secured it. "Oh, yes, Master…" she murmured.

"No area is off limits, and now she has no idea where I will touch her next."

Brie broke out in giggles when he tickled her feet.

"I enjoy keeping her guessing. She never knows where or what kind of touch she is going to receive. It's like a chess game for me. Every move strategic and purposeful, designed to bring my sub maximum stimulation both physically and mentally."

Sir began stroking her buttocks with his hand. She could hear the smile in his voice when he said, "I particularly enjoy spanking this fine ass of hers."

He caressed her ass again, soothingly, teasingly…

Brie held her breath when he raised his hand, readying herself for the first spank. It came down forcefully but without pain. His swats were slow, solid, and controlled, meant solely to arouse. The warmth of his attention spread across her skin at the point of contact, the impact causing ripples of electricity which went straight to her pussy.

She let out a delighted yelp.

The sensual way Sir spanked her was an orgasmic experience. He knew how to use exactly the right pressure and intensity to make her wet.

Prior to the lesson, he had informed her that she was not allowed to come. By the time she was quivering with the need for release, Sir took off the blindfold and switched things up.

"As I said before, even during punishment, a sub should cherish their Master's touch."

The sub who had questioned him on it before shook his head in disbelief.

"I will give you an example, but I will preface it by saying this. Punishments should never be given in the heat of anger. A Dom must wait until they can deliver the punishment with clarity and purpose."

He looked at the group as a whole. "As a submissive, you may not realize that punishments are an essential part of a Dom's duty and are just as important as rewards."

Sir placed his hand on Brie's shoulder. "Punishment is meant to support your sub in their growth and to strengthen the trust and bond between you."

"I don't understand," the sub stated, sounding desperate. Brie could hear the pain in his voice and knew this was a difficult topic for him to hear. She could only imagine what scars he must carry from his past.

Sir did not reprimand him for blurting out. "What is your name?"

The sub lowered his eyes, muttering, "My Dom called me 'piggy' but my given name is Ralph."

Sir nodded. "Ralph, it is important that you understand, so let me explain further."

He turned back to Brie. "Do you remember that time you had to kneel on rice as punishment?"

Brie had never forgotten the excruciating pain of the rice. "I do, Master."

"Did you understand why you were being punished at the time?"

"I did."

"After your punishment was over, how did you feel?"

"I was grateful, Master."

"Why?"

She smiled at him. "I knew I was fully forgiven. Your punishment was a gift, really. I could move forward without any shame because of my mistake. It was now part of my past."

Sir addressed the group again. "After a punishment, a sub should feel empowered, with a full understanding of what they did wrong so they can take action without further guilt."

When Ralph grimaced, Sir asked, "What are you thinking?"

"My Dom found fault in everything I did, Sir Davis. I lived in fear of the next punishment."

Sir looked at him with compassion. "Although there are plenty of partners who enjoy the Disciplinarian/brat dynamic, it has to be something both partners find pleasurable. I would venture to say that, in your case, you were not serving under a true Dominant. Abuse of power is not a part of BDSM."

Ralph nodded, looking somewhat vindicated.

Sir continued, "Let me demonstrate what a punishment would look like for a simple infraction."

Focusing his attention back on Brie, he asked, "Téa, do you understand why you are being punished?"

"Yes, Master."

Sir then told the group, "To verify that my sub truly understands, I ask her to explain it to me. A simple yes will not suffice."

"Why are you being punished, téa?"

Brie thought back to the last time she was punished while driving to the Submissive Training Center and used that as her example.

"I failed to keep my eyes forward, Master."

"Correct."

Sir gave her two hard slaps on her ass. The sound of it reverberated in the room. It had a completely different feel to it, which amazed Brie. There was no doubt those swats were meant as punishment as compared to the sensual ones she'd experienced a few minutes before.

"You are forgiven."

Funny thing, those words had a powerful effect on Brie even though this was only a simulation. She looked up at Sir lovingly. "Thank you, Master."

"As you can see, proper punishment is meant to instruct and should match the level of the infraction."

Ralph raised his hand again. When Sir nodded to him, the sub asked, "What if it doesn't?"

"You would need to discuss it with your Dom.

Communication and trust are key to a healthy relationship."

Ralph looked at Sir with gratitude. "Thank you, Sir Davis. I believe I understand now."

"Good," Sir stated.

When Sir placed his hand on Brie's back, she felt a chill run through her. "Téa, you have done well tonight."

Keeping his hand on her, he bent down and picked up her clothes. He helped her into them while he explained to the students, "I feel strongly that you will gain more from speaking to my submissive."

While she dressed, Baron grabbed two chairs so Brie and Sir could sit comfortably while they answered questions.

"Candy, would you get Brie a glass of water?" Sir asked.

Candy stood up and bowed to him. "It would be my pleasure, Sir Davis."

Sir escorted Brie to the chair and sat down beside her. "Feel free to ask us anything. But, like me, my submissive reserves the right not to answer any question she is uncomfortable with."

Brie smiled at the students. She felt like a goddess under Sir's attentive care. The two of them spent the next hour answering a plethora of questions, none of which made her uncomfortable in the least.

One of the subs asked Brie if Sir was the exception rather than the rule as a Dominant. It was then that Brie was able to share her experience of being under the care of Master Anderson, Tono, and Rytsar. She explained that the men used completely different methods as Dominants, but each was equally nurturing and respectful to her as a sub.

"I must say, being a student of the Submissive Training Center, I was surrounded by Dominants who took pride in their roles." She glanced over at Candy, remembering when they first met on the commuter train. "There weren't any wannabes there."

Candy smiled at her and nodded. "Unfortunately, there are a lot of them out in the world." She turned her attention to the group, her eyes flashing with knowledge and pain. "Knowing what to expect from a Dom will give you the tools you need to avoid the wannabes in the future. You never have to give your submission to the unworthy *ever* again."

The authority in Candy's statement hung in the room, giving Brie goosebumps.

Talking with the other subs on such an intimate level reminded her of her days back at the Submissive Training Center when she was part of the "Three Musketeers" with Lea and Mary.

It was empowering to visit all those feelings again.

Gentle Release

Baron waited until the last student left before slapping Sir on the back. "That was truly an inspired lesson, Sir Davis."

Sir reached out to Brie, who melted into his embrace. "It was an honor for us to be a part of the community you've created here." He glanced at Captain and Candy. "We're grateful to all three of you."

"I appreciate how easily you adapted to the needs of our students, meeting them where they are at emotionally," Baron said with admiration. "You would have been right to reprimand Ralph for his interruption during your demonstration."

"I saw no need. He was genuinely concerned and needed assurance, not reproach. It's obvious how difficult the subject matter was for him. His emotional scars will take time to heal, and I knew keeping to a strict protocol would only have set him back."

"Very astute of you, Sir Davis," Captain stated.

"Sir is an incredible instructor," Brie gushed, staring up at him.

Sir's lips twitched. "'Competent' would be more accurate."

It charmed Brie how humble he was.

"I agree with Brie," Candy exclaimed. "It couldn't have gone any better. I hope you both will consider doing another session with our group in the near future."

Sir glanced at Brie. "I'm certain that can be arranged."

Feeling a deep level of contentment, Brie leaned against Sir just before a big yawn overtook her.

"Although I would enjoy discussing this further, it's been an eventful evening and I need to get my submissive home," Sir told them, looking at Brie tenderly.

"Let me see you both to the door," Baron insisted, walking them out. He shook Sir's hand firmly. "You've made an impact on our student tonight. Thank you."

On the drive home, Brie was silent as she relived every detail of the night's lesson.

"Are you okay, babygirl?" Sir asked with concern.

She giggled. "I'm just flying on an emotional high, Sir."

He smiled, his eyes flashing with satisfaction. "It was exhilarating."

"I had no idea how rewarding tonight would be!"

"I've missed that level of interaction with students," Sir admitted.

Brie turned to stare at him. "Tonight has left me feeling so empowered, Sir. To be able to help other subs is extremely gratifying. At least we still have five weeks before the baby arrives."

"I appreciate your enthusiasm, babygirl," he replied, placing his hand on her stomach. "But it's important that we not overtax your body."

When she frowned in disappointment, he added, "However, I'm certain we can squeeze in one more session before the baby arrives."

She grinned. "That would make me happy, Sir." Glancing down at her stomach, she shook her head. "It's kind of strange not knowing if we will be meeting our little girl or little boy next month."

"It definitely adds a new element to the experience, but I wouldn't want it any other way."

She glanced at Sir, overcome with happiness. "Being able to experience every part of this pregnancy with you has been pure heaven."

He caressed her cheek while keeping one hand firmly on the wheel. "I cannot express what it means to me, babygirl."

When they arrived home, Sir helped Brie out of his Lotus before giving her a command.

"Kneel by the Tantra chair while I select a tool."

Brie nodded, eager to rekindle the flames he'd ignited during their lesson. "Would you like me to undress, Master?"

He surprised her when he answered, "No."

Intrigued, she headed into their bedroom to the Tantra chair and eased herself down to the floor fully clothed.

"Keep your eyes lowered," he directed when he entered the room. He then called out the code for the electronic lock.

She watched covertly as the door to their secret room swung open and Sir disappeared inside. Brie waited breathlessly while he took his time selecting a tool.

She kept her head bowed as he had commanded, even though she was dying to know what he had chosen.

When he returned, he placed a hand on her shoulder. "Do not move."

Sir caressed her breasts with the instrument. With her head lowered, she was able to see he held a leather crop in his hand. However, the tongue was ornately decorated on one side with lace and satin ties in the crisscross pattern of a corset. Although she was familiar with this type of instrument, the tool was a new one in his arsenal.

He teased both of her breasts, causing her nipples to instantly harden. It had been a long time since he'd used an instrument while she was fully dressed. There was something so erotic about the unexpected element and it made her whole body quiver.

Damn, Sir knew how to constantly surprise her!

He slid the crop upwards toward her throat, caressing her jawline with it. Her skin tingled wherever the leather tongue made contact, sending a cascade of shivers down her spine.

Placing the crop's tongue under her chin, he lifted her head. "You are mine, téa."

Her pussy contracted in pleasure hearing the possessive tone of his voice.

"Yes, Master."

Moving her hair over one shoulder so he would have better access, he moved his attention to her back. Just as he had with the front, he trailed the crop lightly down her spine, sending pleasant chills through her body.

It seemed unreal that he could make her gushing wet with just the light touch of the crop. "Oh, Master…"

His low chuckle turned her on even more.

Sir spanked both of her butt cheeks with the crop before grabbing her throat with one hand and sliding the crop underneath the collar of her blouse with the other. Goosebumps rose on her skin when she felt the sensual caress of the leather.

Giving in to it, Brie closed her eyes when the crop slid under her bra and touched her hard nipple. Brie let out a moan of desperation and pleasure, her pussy aching in need for him. The intimacy of his touch through the use of an object helped enhance the experience for her.

Sir stopped for a moment to unbutton the front of her blouse. She held her breath as it fell away, exposing her breasts.

"You are a cinema, téa. I could stare at you for hours…" he murmured lustfully.

Brie smiled to herself, remembering the song he used to play when he placed her in sensual poses and admired her for long periods of time while they were abstaining from sex in preparation for the honeymoon. She was supremely grateful it was not the case tonight.

Sir continued to tease her with the crop, using it as an extension of his fingers. It was an otherworldly experience, and Brie completely surrendered to his seductive caress.

Eventually, he removed her blouse and bra altogether, wanting full access to her skin.

"Hands behind your back," he ordered.

Brie immediately obeyed and was treated to more teasing as he lightly slapped each breast with the crop. His intention was not to sting the skin but to warm it with the instrument.

When he was satisfied with her state of arousal, he ran the crop down her round belly and slipped it under her skirt, rubbing her pussy through her panties. "I can smell how wet you are, téa."

She nodded without shame. "You make me that way, Master."

Sir knew exactly how to play her body. With Brie having already experienced his sensual spanking during the lesson, she was primed and ready for him to take her.

Lightly rapping the crop against her thigh, he moved dangerously close to her pussy again. The thrill of it sent a cascade of chills through her body that traveled straight to her groin.

Brie was desperate for him and moaned seductively in invitation.

He let out a low growl. "Not yet."

She bit her lip to prevent herself from voicing her disappointment, burning with an unquenchable need to be pounded by him.

"Everything you feel plays on your face," he gently teased.

She looked up at him, risking punishment. "I can't hide it. I was made to be claimed by you."

Brie saw the flash of longing in his eyes and knew she'd hit a chink in his armor. Sir was a man of extreme control, but even he had his limits. She could feel his need to ravage her, but he was determined to deny himself a little longer.

Oh, to have the power to make her Master as crazy as he made her was exhilarating!

As punishment, he spanked her ass with the crop, but it only incited delightful tingles that traveled to her pussy, making her moan. Her cries of pleasure must have had a primal effect on him because he suddenly barked, "Stand, téa."

Sir helped Brie to her feet and removed the last of her clothing so she was completely naked before him.

Instead of claiming Brie, he stepped back to gaze at her. "I am in awe as I stand here, looking at you. This exquisite vessel which brings me such pleasure also carries my child. I want you to know that I cherish your body."

A warm flush crept over her chest as she stood before his admiring gaze. "Thank you, Master."

"I must confess—I cannot resist your intoxicating smell any longer."

Her pussy pulsated in response to his fervent desire. "Take me, Master," she pleaded.

He raised an eyebrow.

"Please…" she begged.

He walked back to her. Grabbing her throat with a possessive hold, he pulled her head back and demanded, "What do you want?"

"I want you inside me…" she cried in desperation. "Deep."

"How deep?"

"As deep as you please, Master."

Sir grunted, "So be it."

Her pussy gushed with wetness now that his claiming was close at hand.

Brie bit her lip when he ordered her to climb onto the tantra chair. She heard him unbuckle his belt and unzip his pants. He then positioned himself behind her.

She purred lustfully when she felt the head of his cock rub against her swollen pussy.

"Damn…" he growled. "You're so fucking wet."

"I am, Master," she agreed, pressing her slick mound against his shaft.

He immediately slapped her on the ass, the echo reverberating through the room. "Stay perfectly still. I want you to fully experience the thrust when I take you."

"Yes, Master." She closed her eyes so she could devote all of her attention to his passionate claiming.

Sir positioned his cock, letting out a deep-throated groan as he slowly thrust his shaft into her pussy all the way to the hilt.

Brie let out a strangled cry as she took the full length of his cock. He fisted her hair, pressing himself even deeper into her. The challenge of it heightened her arousal.

"Your body is desperate for me."

She moaned in agreement, her body shuddering with satisfaction after receiving what she had been craving all evening.

"Do you want it gentle or rough?"

"Rough," she cried, imagining the hard pounding she was about to enjoy.

Sir's low chuckle filled the room. "What happened to your desire for my pleasure, téa?"

She immediately amended her answer. "Only if it pleases you, Master."

Instead of rough sex, Sir was gentle with her. Each

stroke was deep and challenging, but he thrust into her slowly, making it a sensual exchange that drew her even closer to him. Each measured stroke of his shaft stimulated her G-spot, making her thighs tremble uncontrollably.

"You're close," he murmured in her ear.

"So close…"

"Would you like to come?"

She purred, "Only if it pleases you."

Sir leaned down, biting her neck. "It does…"

Brie whimpered in pleasure, submitting to the flames he had stoked so meticulously over the entire evening.

The orgasm Brie experienced was uniquely strong but tender, her pussy clenching his shaft with each pulse as she came. It wasn't until the last powerful surge passed that she felt his cock stiffen inside her just before he filled her with his essence.

Brie moaned when he came, entranced by his control and dedication to their mutual pleasure. Afterward, he wrapped an arm around her and kissed the bruised area left by his teeth.

"I love you, Master," she sighed, feeling completely satisfied, physically and emotionally.

"And I love you, my fuckable goddess."

Brie received a box from Russia a couple of days later. She opened it up and found a card and two stuffed animals.

The card read:

The horse is for moye solntse *and the bear is for the babe. They are to be played at bedtime.*

There was also a box wrapped in red paper addressed to Sir. Curious, Brie opened the card attached:

You are not to open the red box, radost moya. *It is for your Master's eyes only.*

Brie laughed, now even more curious about the red box. "Wicked sadist…"

She had no idea why Rytsar wanted Hope to play with her new toy only at bedtime, but didn't question it. However, her daughter would not be denied once she saw the white horse.

Hope held up her hands for it as if she knew the gift was from her *dyadya*.

Grabbing it by one of the hooves, Hope ran off, dragging the horse across the floor with Shadow following behind her.

Out of the blue, Brie heard Rytsar's voice fill the room, *"Moye solntse…"*

She turned to see Hope staring at the horse with wide eyes as the stuffed animal spoke to her. "I wish you sweet dreams tonight. May you ride the clouds of sleep on your brilliant steed and return to Earth safe and sound knowing your *dyadya* loves you."

Hope stared at the stuffed animal in surprise for several seconds before crushing it in a tight hug. Standing beside her, Shadow gazed at the toy intently, quickly swishing his tail back and forth in a playful manner.

The two of them were so cute that Brie snatched her

phone to take a quick picture to share with Rytsar.

Now understanding the significance of the stuffed animals, Brie took the brown teddy bear out of the box. Placing it against her stomach, she pressed the paw, and Rytsar's gruff but soothing voice came from the bear.

"Little one, it is time to go to bed..." Brie smiled when he began signing the Russian lullaby his mother had sung to him as a boy. Pressing the bear tighter against her belly, Brie closed her eyes as she lost herself in the warm timbre of his song.

"...the sun's gone to sleep. Close your eyes and I'll rock you gently..."

Her eyes popped open when she suddenly felt the baby move as if reacting to Rytsar's voice. Looking down, she saw her daughter toddling toward her, dragging the horse. She wrapped a chubby little arm around Brie's leg and looked up. "*Dyadya.*"

Brie grinned. "Yes, sweet pea, *dyadya* is singing."

Brie shook her head in amazement. Despite the thousands of miles that separated them, Rytsar had found a meaningful way to remain a part of both children's lives.

She glanced at the red box again, now more curious than ever, wondering what gift was contained inside.

A Little Lea Time

When Sir informed Brie that he had not been given permission to divulge the contents of the red box, she decided to take matters into her own hands and texted Rytsar.

Sir just told me he can't share what's in the box. How is that fair?

All is fair in passion and pain.

She whimpered as she quickly keyed in her rebuttal.

You're cruel, Rytsar.

Thank you.

Brie could just imagine him laughing as he texted his response.

Although she knew there was nothing she could say to get that sexy sadist to change his mind, she made one last try.

I'll make it worth your while…

Your suffering is all I require, radost moya.

She giggled despite her frustration.

Then it hit her. The box might simply be a ruse designed to drive her crazy. He knew her curious nature well and how much she struggled with patience. What if this was just a cruel prank?

Is there anything in the box?

When he didn't answer, she realized he was toying with her.

Fine. I will suffer, Rytsar, but only because you will it. And that pleases me.

Brie smirked as she put down the phone. In need of a distraction, she asked Sir if she could spend a couple of hours with Lea. She missed spending quality girl time with her best friend.

"Why don't you invite her here?" Sir suggested.

"What an excellent idea."

Lea jumped at the chance to hang at the beach and was there within the hour.

As soon as Brie opened the door, Lea stared at her belly in shock. "Whoa, that baby is about to pop! Should we move your baby shower up?"

Brie laughed. "Nope. I still have more than four weeks to go."

Lea shook her head but continued to stare at her stomach as she walked inside.

"Is there a problem?" Brie laughed, amused by Lea's sudden interest in her belly.

She blushed. "I didn't mean to be rude, Stinky Cheese. I'm just trying to imagine what it's like."

"It's uncomfortable when you get to this point in the pregnancy," Brie admitted, rubbing her belly. "But it's worth it. I'm actually looking forward to going full term this time. It'll be nice to have a normal pregnancy, especially since this will be our last."

Lea looked surprised. "You're not planning to have

any more?"

"This is it for us. Girl or boy, this little one is the last Davis for our little family."

Lea pouted. "That actually makes me kinda sad."

"Why?" Brie chuckled.

"You and Sir make such beautiful babies."

Brie put an arm around Lea. "I bet you will, too."

Lea's blush grew a deeper shade of red. "Nope…not going to happen."

"Still weirded out by the whole pregnancy thing, huh?"

"I totally love the fucking part of the process," she stated enthusiastically, then shuddered. "But the idea of having an alien in my stomach for nine months gives me the heebie-jeebies."

"Does Hunter want kids?"

Lea giggled. "It's not like we talk about that kind of stuff, silly."

Brie raised her eyebrows. "Oh, so you two aren't serious?"

"I'm not saying that…"

"So, you are?" Brie prodded, grinning.

To avoid answering the question, Lea blurted, "Hey, do you know why babies born on holidays are more likely to be little girls?"

Sir walked up and surprised them both when he willingly took the plunge, "Tell me, Ms. Taylor, why are they more likely to be girls?"

Lea's eyes grew wide when she was confronted by this unexpected exchange with Sir and squeaked, "Because there is no mail delivery on holidays."

Sir stared at her with a stoic expression. "I see."

His serious tone made Lea's bad joke even funnier to Brie and she burst out laughing.

Lea gave her a dubious look before joining in her laughter, then hip bumping her. "Good one, huh?"

"Good would be an exaggeration, Ms. Taylor. Mildly entertaining? Possibly…" Sir gave Brie a private wink.

Lea stared at him, uncertain how to respond.

He broke the silence by informing Brie, "I'm taking Hope into my office so you can spend time alone together."

"Thank you, Sir," Brie answered, bowing gratefully to him.

"Yes, thank you, Sir Davis," Lea murmured uncomfortably.

As they were walking outside to lay out on the beach, Lea asked, her voice was little better than a strangled cry, "Does he really hate my jokes?"

Brie wrapped an arm around her and laughed. "No, I'm sure he doesn't."

"That's not very reassuring."

Brie leaned over and whispered, "Sir winked at me when he was talking to you. I think he was just having fun."

"Oh!" Lea's entire face suddenly brightened. "Well, I like a good challenge. I'll just hit him with my best baby joke before I leave. I'll make him laugh, just you wait!"

"That's the spirit," Brie encouraged her, giving Lea a playful punch on the shoulder. There was no one in the world like Lea—she was a breath of pure joy.

Lea whipped off her t-shirt, exposing her large boobs, which were straining against her tiny polka dot bikini. "How do you like my new swimsuit?"

Brie stared at her chest. "All I see are boobs, girl-friend."

"Perfect, right?" She twisted back and forth to show off every angle.

Slipping off her own shirt, Brie heard Lea whistle appreciatively. "Well now, would you look at that? Your boobs are humungous, Stinky Cheese!"

Brie looked down at her breasts. "I suppose they are. Just one of the perks of pregnancy."

"Well, at least there's *one* positive thing about housing a little alien."

"Besides the miracle of life?" Brie teased.

Lea crinkled her nose. "You know, Brie, I'd make a joke about newborns right now, but…" She glanced to the side playfully, pouting her lips. "The delivery would be too painful."

Brie groaned. "That was awful, Lea."

"So bad you loved it. Am I right?" Lea threw her fist in the air in a silent cheer before lying down on her beach towel. "You know I have another baby joke for you, right?"

Brie grinned as she lay down beside her. "I'd be offended if you didn't."

"Do you know how warm a baby is at birth?"

Brie snorted. "How would you know? You've never been pregnant."

Lea batted the air with her hand like a cat. "Come on! You have to play along, Stinky Cheese."

Brie rolled her eyes good-naturedly. "Fine. How warm?"

"Womb temperature," Lea answered, bursting into a fit of giggles.

Brie looked up at the sky, shaking her head. "Where do you even find these?"

"I have a secret vault of funny goodness. If the apocalypse happened tomorrow, I could supply you with a steady stream of jokes for at least two years."

Brie cringed. "That's actually kind of scary to think about."

"I know! I'll be like the ultimate secret weapon, unleashing my jokes on the enemy to distract them while the infantry marches in from behind."

"Sounds like you have the apocalypse all figured out."

"Yep! I plan to save the world—one joke at a time."

Brie reached out, squeezing Lea's hand. "I love your warrior spirit."

Lea grinned. "Don't you worry, Brie. I'll protect you and the little alien you've got there."

Brie closed her eyes, caressing her stomach as she talked to the baby. "Don't listen to Aunt Lea. Despite her bad jokes and alien references, she's a wonderful human."

She lay there reveling in the warmth of the sun on her skin and the soothing sound of the waves, content to be lying beside her best friend. The two lay together in pleasant silence for a long time.

Lea sighed. "I miss our girl time."

"Yeah, we should do this more often," Brie agreed.

The comfortable silence resumed until Lea said, "I'm worried about Mary."

"Me, too…" Brie confessed. Her heart started to race. She was frightened that she might say something to Lea and accidentally break Mary's trust. Not wanting to take the chance, she diverted the conversation back to Lea. "What was it like living with her?"

"Oh, Mary's a real peach," Lea chuckled sarcastically. "I get why she feels the need to make snarky comments about Hunter and me—that Greg of hers is a total fuckbucket. What I don't understand is why she went back to the creep…" She shook her head angrily. "It doesn't make any sense to me."

"I don't think anyone knows what Mary's going through because she's so good at putting up barriers to keep us out."

"Well, she's only hurting herself." Lea's tone grew softer. "She's changed, Brie… There is a soft, squishy side to her now under all those porcupine quills. Even Hunter noticed it."

Brie turned her head to look Lea in the eyes. "Mary's a lot kinder than she lets on."

Lea snorted with amusement. "Who would have guessed on that first day at the Training Center? She was so full of herself. God, I just wanted to smack her!"

Brie chuckled, remembering their first day. "She definitely earned her name as 'Blonde Nemesis.'"

"I thought you were freakin' crazy to invite her to have drinks with us that first time."

Brie shrugged. "It felt wrong to leave her out."

Lea clicked her tongue. "She sure doesn't make it easy to like her, does she? Still, she sees things I don't see—especially when it came to Liam…" Frowning, Lea glanced at Brie.

Brie could tell her friend was privately reliving the hell she'd gone through with Liam.

Lea shrugged. "That's why I agreed to let Mary stay

with me when she asked. Even though she's a total pain in the butt to live with, I always know she's got my back no matter what."

Tears pricked Brie's eyes. "I feel the same, Lea."

Lea's eyes suddenly flashed with resentment. "That's why it pissed me off so bad when she told me she was going back to that asshole. How can you feel sorry for someone who keeps making bad choices over and over again? I have to admit, Brie, I lost respect for Mary when she went crawling back to Greg this time."

Brie wanted to tell Lea what was really happening, that she only went back to Holloway to protect Brie.

But she'd vowed to keep Mary's secret.

Rather than break Mary's confidence, Brie said miserably, "Maybe there'll come a day when she'll tell us what's really going on."

"I hope so," Lea sighed. "But I'm convinced that girl is a train wreck waiting to happen—and I don't want to be around when it does."

Brie's heart skipped a beat, feeling terrified for Mary. "God, I hope that day never comes…"

When it finally came time for Lea to head back home, she knocked on the doorframe of Sir's office.

"Sir Davis, before I leave, I just wanted to warn you not to play Scrabble around Hope."

He turned, looking at Lea strangely. "What are you talking about, Ms. Taylor?"

"If she eats a bunch of those tiles, it could spell disaster."

Silence filled the room.

When she failed to get a reaction from him, Lea followed it up by playing imaginary drums and saying, "Ba dum tss…" to emphasize it was a joke.

Sir raised an eyebrow and then glanced at Hope. "My daughter is not impressed. But, it was a valiant effort, Ms. Taylor."

Lea turned to Brie, who was struggling hard not to laugh. The fact that Lea had the nerve to hit Sir up with such a bad joke was courageous—and extremely foolhardy.

"He's going to be a tough nut to crack," Lea confessed when they were out of his earshot.

Brie couldn't hold back any longer and burst out laughing, "I can't believe you just did that, Lea."

"I told you I would."

"Well…I expected that you had a better joke for Sir."

"The joke isn't the problem, Stinky Cheese." She put her arm around Brie's shoulder. "I hate to tell you this, but Sir Davis has an underdeveloped sense of humor."

Brie's eyes widened. She was amused that Lea was placing the blame on Sir. "You really think he's the problem?"

Lea hugged her compassionately. "Don't feel bad. Your Master is exceptional in a lot of other areas."

She couldn't tell if Lea was pulling her leg or being serious.

"Oh!" Brie suddenly gasped, pressing her hand against her stomach.

Lea frowned. "What's wrong?"

"Nothing. The baby's just being super active right now."

Lea bit her lip for a moment before asking, "Mind if I feel it?"

Brie was surprised by the request. "You sure you want to? I remember how creeped out you were the last time."

Lea shrugged before tentatively placing her hand on Brie's belly.

Brie guided her hand to the area where the baby was moving. The moment Lea felt a kick, she immediately pulled her hand back. "Wow! That was a really strong kick. Does it hurt?"

"No. However, it does get uncomfortable at times."

Lea placed her hand back on Brie's stomach and stood there with a wistful look on her face while she felt the baby's movements. When she caught Brie staring at her, she removed her hand and laughed self-consciously. "You've got a feisty little alien there."

Brie only nodded.

She was certain Lea had been daydreaming about what a little version of Hunter might look like. She remembered when she used to do that with Sir back in her training days, and it made her smile.

The Red Box

The Reynolds insisted on taking Hope overnight. They wanted to give the two children quality "cousin time" together. Knowing how important it was, Brie eagerly agreed. Besides, it would give her an entire evening to delve into her work.

Lately, she had been trying to solve a mystery concerning Alonzo. She had come across a reference about a private concert for an important client in Mancini's black book. But she hadn't found any record of who it was for or where this private performance took place.

Brie felt certain if she had access to the letters, she would find the information she was looking for. As it was, she had to rely solely on her ability to google it, and she hadn't been successful in finding anything yet.

Armed with a variety of new keywords, she settled in for a long session of sleuthing.

Sir called up from downstairs, "Durov is on the phone."

Brie jumped up from her desk and hurried downstairs to join him, hoping Rytsar had some good news. It wasn't until she made it to the bottom of the stairs that she noticed the mischievous glint in Sir's eyes.

"We'll be taking the call in the bedroom."

She smiled as she followed him, wondering what the two Doms had planned. Putting the phone on speaker, Sir stated, "She's here."

"Excellent," Rytsar replied, his rich Russian accent filling the room.

"What's going on?" she asked Sir.

The Russian answered, "I have missed you, *radost moya*."

Her heart squeezed with love for him. "I've missed you too, Rytsar."

Sir held up the red box.

Finally! She was about to find out what was in it...

He lifted the lid and pulled out a dildo that looked suspiciously like Rytsar's cock. He pressed a button and a trail of purple lights raced up the side of the phallus.

Entranced, Brie stared at it as he set the instrument on the nightstand. Sir then turned off the lights in the room so the only illumination came from the full moon outside.

"I'll begin by taking her clothes off," Sir announced in a low voice.

"Excellent," Rytsar growled.

Sir walked to Brie, brushing his hand against her cheek. That light touch sent tingles through her body. He turned her around and slowly unzipped the back of her dress, then brushed the material off her shoulders.

As Sir undressed her, he detailed exactly what he was doing for Rytsar. When he freed her breasts from her lacy bra, Rytsar commanded, "Squeeze them for me, comrade. Tease her nipples."

Sir obliged, cupping both breasts in his firm hands and gently squeezing them as he rolled her hard nipples between his fingertips.

Brie moaned in pleasure, leaning back against him.

Sir described his actions as he wrapped his hand around her throat and tilted her head back. "I'm going to kiss her now…"

Brie parted her lips as he claimed her mouth, inviting his sensual embrace.

His possessive hold on her throat enhanced the kiss as he explored her mouth with his tongue. Her moans grew louder, her pussy aching for him.

"Feel between her legs, *moy droog*. Tell me how wet she is."

Sir slipped his hand under her panties and swiped his finger over her wet clit. "She is juicy with need."

Rytsar's low, guttural laughter filled the room. "I can only imagine. How does she taste?"

Sir slipped his finger inside her and then ran his finger over her bottom lip before tasting her for himself. "I'll let her answer."

Brie licked her lip and replied, "Salty sweet."

Sir claimed her lips again, her womanly juices mixing with the intoxicating taste of him.

"You will need to pound her hard tonight. I want her to taste her own come."

Sir growled deep in his chest, obviously liking the idea.

He guided her to the bed, telling Rytsar, "You will want to apply the instrument."

Brie had no idea what he was talking about.

Anticipating her question, Rytsar said, "I'm placing the electronic stroker on my shaft, which is linked to the dildo I sent you, *radost moya*. It will simulate whatever you do to it."

Brie stared at the phallus in excitement. "Ooh…we're having virtual sex?"

"*Da.*"

Sir whispered, "Take the phallus and stroke it."

She picked it up from the nightstand and stroked the length of it with one hand. Rytsar's manly groan filled the room.

It was like magic, being able to bring him pleasure thousands of miles away.

Sir told Rytsar that he was positioning her against the bed. Sir had Brie press her thighs against the edge. Laying a pillow on the bed to support her torso, Sir instructed her to bend over and lay her chest on the pillow while still holding the dildo with both hands.

He then grabbed a towel from the bathroom and carefully placed it under her feet. Brie bit her lip, excited by the fact he was preparing to make her gush with come.

Laying her torso against the pillow, she grasped the phallus tightly in her hands. She was rewarded with Rytsar's groan of pleasure.

When she kissed the tip of it, he growled and commanded, "Suck me, *radost moya*."

Brie wrapped her lips around the head of the shaft and began sucking.

"I can feel the pressure of your mouth," he said huskily.

Curious as to just how much he could feel, she

swirled her tongue around the hood of the dildo."

"*Blyad…*" he groaned in appreciation.

Realizing how sensitive the instrument was, Brie slowly took the length of it down her throat. Hearing his low grunts of appreciation made her pussy even wetter.

Sir took advantage of it, slipping his rigid shaft into her. "Fuck, she's hot."

"I can imagine," Rytsar replied lustfully.

Lying against the bed in the dark, Brie imagined Rytsar was physically there with them, playing out the scene. She continued to deep throat the shaft while Sir pushed the full length of his cock into her. He changed the angle of his thrusts to ensure the head of his cock rubbed against her G-spot.

Brie pressed her teeth into the shaft around the ridge of the cock and heard Rytsar suck in his breath. "Do you like that?"

"*Da…*" he growled hoarsely.

While Brie concentrated on providing Rytsar with the best blowjob of his life, Sir was equally set on making her gush. Her pussy was already super wet, making a delightfully juicy sound every time he thrust into her. Even Rytsar could hear it.

"Is she close, *moy droog?*"

"Yes," he answered, smacking her on the ass.

It was true. Each stroke of his cock was bringing her closer to orgasm. It didn't take long before she was whimpering in need as she sucked on Rytsar's shaft.

The Russian let out a low chuckle. "I can feel that."

It was exhilarating to have this intimate connection with him after being apart for so long. She deep throated the shaft again, making little up and down movements to tighten her throat around the phallus.

His guttural cry of pleasure sent her over the edge and her pussy contracted powerfully as a gush of wetness covered Sir's cock.

"She's coming hard," he informed Rytsar. Sir remained still as her inner muscles squeezed his shaft in rhythmic waves of pleasure.

"Put me inside," Rytsar ordered through gritted teeth.

Sir immediately pulled out and Brie slipped the phallus into her wet pussy as the last pulses of her orgasm caressed it. Hearing Rytsar groan as he came caused her pussy to contract tightly around the toy, intensifying the experience for both of them.

She pulled out the dildo and licked the head of the shaft, murmuring, "My come tastes like sweet water, Rytsar."

Sir let out a lustful growl, filling her with his cock in a solid thrust. Leaning down he growled, "I'm going to make you come even harder."

Brie held her breath as he ramped up the speed of his thrusts. Rather than fucking her deeper, he concentrated his efforts on stimulating her G-spot.

"Oh God, oh God..." she whimpered as her thighs began to shake.

"Come for me, téa," Sir commanded.

Her body responded to his command, stiffening as the tidal wave raced toward her. This orgasm was so powerful, she momentarily lost herself in it.

Sir grunted in satisfaction as he knelt on the floor next to the bed and buried his mouth in her mound, licking her freshly-come pussy.

"Fuck, you taste good…"

Brie's thighs continued to tremble as Sir repositioned himself and thrust his shaft into her again. The sexy sound of skin slapping against skin filled their bedroom as he pumped his seed into her, enjoying his own release.

Her cries of pleasure came out in mewing gasps as she floated on the sub high caused by the unique three-some.

"Did *radost moya* survive?" Rytsar teased.

Sir swept a strand of hair from her face and smiled. "She's still flying."

"Good."

Sir joined Brie on the bed, wrapping his arms around her. "It was a spirited fucking."

Rytsar chuckled. "*Da.* I feel as if *radost moya* sucked the life out of me."

Brie nodded. She had felt the same intensity with Sir.

"I'd say your new toy was a success," Sir murmured, kissing Brie on the neck.

"Agreed, comrade."

Brie let out a sigh of contentment, snuggling against Sir as she enjoyed the pleasurable haze of her sub high while listening to the two men talk.

"*Moy droog*, while I was impressed by the number of donuts you sent, I was not prepared to receive a new box every week. Are you trying to make me fat?"

Sir chuckled. "I figured you could learn how to share."

"Never! I've had to increase my exercise to account for them."

"That's your solution?"

"When it comes to donuts, I have no wish to share,"

he growled.

Sir snorted. "You remind me of a dog with three tennis balls in its mouth."

"While it may be uncomfortable, *moy droog*, you're looking at one contented animal."

"You or the dog?"

Brie could imagine Rytsar's smirk when he answered, "Both."

"Would you like me to stop the shipments, then?"

"*Nyet!* I count on my daily Blueberry Bourbon Basil donut to keep me sane."

Sir began stroking Brie's hair, a smile playing on his lips. "Fine, I'll keep the supply chain coming."

"Good." Rytsar suddenly let out a frustrated sigh. "Sadly, I must go. I need to shower before my meeting."

Brie glanced out the window at the night sky. His words had reminded her of the vast time zone difference between them.

"What is the meeting about?" Sir asked.

"We're finalizing plans for the construction of the containment facility. I'll send the blueprints for your approval once we conclude the meeting."

Brie lifted her head. "Construction is about to begin?"

"*Da*, it is," he stated proudly.

A sense of peace suddenly washed over her. "I can't tell you how happy that makes me."

"Sweet dreams, *radost moya…*"

After Rytsar ended the call, Brie gazed into Sir's eyes with a sense of growing relief. "It's really happening, Sir."

"It is, babygirl." He kissed her on the forehead and began stroking her hair again. "You can rest easy now."

Perfect Day

B rie woke up the next morning overflowing with excitement. Unable to contain it, she quietly slid out of bed and slipped her clothes on.

Heading outside, she walked barefoot in the sand to the water's edge and watched the waves gently roll in around her feet.

She attributed her sense of well-being to the knowledge that the construction of the facility was about to begin. Having Lilly safely locked up and receiving medical care for her mental issues would ease Brie's fears and allow her to fully embrace the birth that was coming. Ever since she was confronted with the situation at the convent and was forced to deal with Lilly's deteriorating mental health, Brie had been subconsciously on alert every minute of every day.

Now, the pressure of those fears had an end date. Once Lilly was transferred, Brie could relax. Knowing that time was coming soon brought her a feeling of immense relief.

When she felt the baby kick, Brie looked down at her

stomach and smiled. "I can't wait to meet you, little one. You have a big sister who will look after you, as well as the most amazing daddy." Tears came to her eyes when she imagined the moment when Sir held their baby in his arms for the first time…

It would be breathtakingly beautiful.

The instant Kylie's death came to mind, Brie pushed it away. "I control my thoughts!" Brie shouted over the waves.

She was determined not to let anything ruin the incredible feeling of peace she was experiencing today. Turning toward the house, she saw Sir standing at their back door, smiling at her.

Her joy increased tenfold as she walked into his open arms.

"You seem especially content this morning. Last night's scene seems to have had a positive effect on you."

"That's part of it, I'm sure." She wrapped her arms around him. "But it's so much more than that, Sir. I feel like I'm flying on cloud nine right now."

He caressed her cheek. "I like seeing you this way, babygirl."

She squeezed him tight, letting out a contented sigh. However, she was so full of energy, she couldn't remain still for long.

"I feel like making some of Nonna's hot chocolate."

"Why not?" Sir chuckled as he escorted her inside.

Brie grinned, thinking of Sir's grandparents as she got out the Italian chocolate and started chopping it into small pieces. "Did you get the blueprints from Rytsar last night?" she called out to Sir.

He walked out of his office with his laptop. "They're right here."

Setting the computer down on the counter, he told her, "Let's wait to look them over together after we enjoy the hot chocolate you're making."

Brie smiled as she stirred the warm milk and watched the chocolate pieces slowly melt into chocolaty goodness. When she glanced up, she caught Sir staring at her. The expression on his face took her breath away—it was full of such tenderness and love that it made her blush with happiness.

He smirked. "I see I can still make you blush, Miss Bennett."

"It's your secret power, Sir…"

He stood up and walked over to her. Tilting her head to one side, Sir kissed her throat, before biting down lightly. Chills coursed through her body and she momentarily forgot herself.

"Keep stirring," he reminded her gently.

Brie came back to her senses and resumed stirring the hot chocolate while Sir got two mugs from the cupboard.

"Let me do the honors," he insisted, taking the small saucepan and pouring an equal amount of the warm chocolate into both.

Sir handed her a mug and escorted her to their back patio where they could drink in privacy while still enjoying the sound of the ocean.

It was the start of a perfect day.

Brie smiled as she sipped the decadent drink and felt the baby kick as if she or he was reacting to the yumminess of it. "I think our little one loves Nonna's chocolate, too."

Sir placed his hand on her stomach and grinned when he felt the baby's hard kick. "This one is certainly active today."

Brie laughed. "I bet she or he is going to be a world-renowned soccer player."

While she sat there, trying to leisurely sip her hot chocolate, Brie had to continually readjust her position because the baby wouldn't stop moving. Finally, she set the mug down, conceding defeat. "I guess the baby likes it a little too much," she giggled. "I better not drink anymore."

Sir looked at her with sympathy and picked up her mug, stating, "Let's check out those blueprints, then."

As Brie was following him inside, she felt a sudden gush of warmth between her legs. The blood drained from her face and she cried, "Sir…"

He turned to see the puddle of water at her feet.

"Not again," Brie whimpered.

Sir instantly took control of the situation. "We've been through this before," he assured her as he escorted her inside.

He immediately called Dr. Glas. "Brianna's water just broke. We're heading to the hospital right now."

Sir then asked her, "How far apart are the contractions?"

She shook her head. "I can't tell…the baby is so active."

"Dr. Glas says he is going to meet us at the hospital."

Brie's bottom lip began to tremble. "I'm scared, Sir."

"Don't be, babygirl. I can get you to the hospital quickly, but if you prefer an ambulance, I'll arrange it."

"No, I'd rather you drive, Sir."

Keeping a calm demeanor, Sir helped Brie dress in fresh clothes and quickly packed an overnight bag for her. As he escorted her to the Lotus, he explained, "I know this isn't easy for you to get in and out of, but she'll get us there much faster."

Brie nodded as she took his hand and he helped her into the vehicle. She'd thought she had seen him drive fast before, but that wasn't even close to how fast he was driving now.

With laser focus, Sir weaved in and out of traffic, punching the gas to the floor whenever there was room. Brie had never been so grateful for the sports car or his ability to drive it past the limits.

Not surprisingly, they soon heard the sound of a blaring siren behind them.

Sir kept his gaze forward and told her, "I'm not stopping. Call 911 and tell them we are headed to the hospital."

She hurriedly grabbed the phone out of her purse, unable to stop her hands from shaking as she dialed the number. Sir rattled off his license plate number when they asked.

"Sir, they say to slow down and let the police car get in front of you so they can escort you to the hospital safely."

Sir growled in frustration but took his foot off the gas so the police vehicle could maneuver around them.

With sirens still blaring, Sir reluctantly followed behind.

Brie reached out and placed her hand on his thigh, needing his physical presence.

Sir did not take his eyes off the road but assured her, "Everything is going to be fine, babygirl."

There was no hint of doubt in his voice, and Brie held onto that as her fears continued to grow. The baby was coming three weeks early—just like Hope.

Brie felt certain the baby was struggling and was the reason it was being so active right now.

What if this baby doesn't survive this…?

Brie gasped, unable to bear the thought, and started to cry.

"Don't," Sir commanded, as he stared straight ahead. "Focus only on the positive."

Brie nodded, squeezing her eyes shut to force the tears back while she focused on her breathing.

I'm here, little one. Daddy is getting us to the hospital as fast as he can so we can meet you.

Brie repeated those words over and over, not allowing herself to think about anything else.

After what seemed like an eternity, Sir pulled up to the hospital entrance where a nurse was waiting for them with a wheelchair.

Sir quickly helped her out of the vehicle and into the wheelchair. "I'll park the car and find you."

"I don't want you to leave me," Brie cried, breaking down in tears.

Sir took her hand and squeezed it. "I'll be as quick as I can, babygirl."

A man walking into the hospital stopped midstride and turned to him. "I'll park the car and leave the keys at the front desk, if you'd like."

Sir hesitated for only a second before handing him the keys. "Thank you. Your name is…?"

"Kyle."

Sir nodded to him before following Brie inside. "Aren't you worried about your car?"

He shook his head. "No. The car means nothing right now."

Brie took his hand and kissed it, strengthened by his uncompromising love.

Once they reached the maternity floor, Brie was rushed to a private room where Dr. Glas was waiting for them. He smiled when he saw her.

"Just like the last one, your babe is anxious to greet the world."

"I'm scared," Brie confessed, unconsciously echoing Kylie's words on the day she died. "There's something's wrong with the baby. I can feel it."

"Let me make that assessment," Dr. Glas stated firmly, asking her to undress. As he helped her onto the examination table and pulled out the stirrups, the doctor met her gaze. "You and your babe will receive the best care, lass."

Brie nodded, trusting him despite her growing panic. She threw a worried glance Sir's way as Dr. Glas placed the fetal heart monitor on her stomach.

The baby's heart rate was erratic, rapidly beating one moment, then slowing way down the next.

Dr. Glas nodded thoughtfully and donned his gloves. He pressed his fingers inside her and smiled when he felt the opening of her cervix. "The good news is you're progressing nicely. However, the babe is in distress. I suspect the cord is wrapped around the neck so we'll fill your womb with additional fluid to relieve any pressure the umbilical cord may be causing."

"Is that dangerous?" Sir asked in concern.

"Not at all, Mr. Davis. It's a simple transfusion of saline solution using a catheter. If the heart rate stabilizes, we can talk about having an epidural."

Dr. Glas winked at Brie, his calm demeanor helping to allay her fears.

The procedure itself was painless, and it didn't take long before the baby's heart rate returned to a steady, consistent beat.

"After the complications with the nuchal cord during your first delivery, I made provisions in case we faced the same scenario with this one," he explained.

Tears of gratitude welled up in Brie's eyes. "Thank you, Dr. Glas."

His smile was genuine, but Brie could see the haunted look in the doctor's eyes. She could tell he was determined to do whatever was necessary to ensure she and the baby made it through the delivery safely.

Brie suddenly grimaced as intense pain enveloped her. Now that the baby was less active, she was fully aware of her contractions.

"I can have the anesthesiologist come in and get started on the epidural for you," Dr. Glas offered.

Brie nodded but, after he left, she confessed to Sir, "Even though I want the epidural, I'm terrified about the idea of having a needle up my spine."

He looked at her with compassion. "You don't have to have it, but remember the pain you endured during Hope's birth."

Brie shuddered, recalling how excruciating it was. "You're right, Sir. I'd rather not have everyone on the floor hear me scream 'I'm not a masochist' this time."

Sir chuckled warmly. "I actually thought it was charming."

Brie blushed, loving his answer.

Sir pulled his phone out of his pocket. "Would you like me to call your parents?"

"Yes! I would love it if they could be here for the birth…" Brie's voice trailed off, suddenly overcome with sadness. "Wait, Sir. Let's call Rytsar first."

Sir nodded, dialing his number instead. "Brother, we wanted you to be the first to know that Brie's in labor."

Sir put the phone on speaker and Brie heard Rytsar cry out, "So soon?"

"Her water broke this morning, so I rushed her to the hospital."

"I wish you could be here with us," Brie told Rytsar, her heart aching because he was so far away.

"I do too, *radost moya*, but know this Russian is beside you in spirit."

She choked back her tears. "I know…"

"Is the babe okay?"

When she hesitated to answer, Rytsar demanded, "What's wrong, Brother?"

Sir told him what had happened, assuring Rytsar the baby's heartbeat was stable, and Brie was progressing well.

Rytsar was silent for a moment. Brie could only imagine how agonizing it must be for him to know there was nothing he could do. "*Radost moya*, I—"

Their call was interrupted by the anesthesiologist entering the room. "I was told you are ready for an epidural, Mrs. Davis."

Brie glanced at Sir, her courage suddenly leaving her.

"I hate to do this to you, but I'll need to call you back. Brie's anesthesiologist just arrived," Sir explained to Rytsar before hanging up.

He placed a reassuring hand on Brie's shoulder before addressing the doctor. "My wife has concerns about the epidural."

The anesthesiologist nodded and pulled up a stool. He sat down to explain the entire procedure in detail to her. "It's completely natural to be concerned about the pain, but I will numb up the area before I insert the needle into your back. You will feel pressure, but it shouldn't be painful."

Brie let out a sigh of relief. "Good."

"If you're ready, I'll get that area numbed up right now."

Brie nodded, then took Sir's hand while the doctor had her lay on her side. She squeezed it tight when she felt the bite and the burn of the initial numbing shot. The doctor rubbed the area for several minutes while a nurse prepared the materials for the epidural.

Brie was too scared to even look at the tray.

Sir kept his eyes on Brie the entire time, his reassuring smile helping her to remain calm. But she immediately tensed when the anesthesiologist said, "This next part may feel strange. I'm going to push the needle between your vertebrae and into your spine. It might feel uncomfortable, but only for a short time."

Brie shut her eyes when she felt the needle slowly enter. It was a completely unsettling feeling, and she had to force herself not to whimper.

But, before she knew it, the nurse was taping the catheter in place. "All done, my dear!"

Brie couldn't believe it and smiled at Sir.

Before the anesthesiologist left, he told her, "I suggest you rest now, while you still can."

Brie nodded, although she knew it would be impossible. She was far too wound up to even think about sleep. However, she took extreme comfort in the sound of her baby's steady heartbeat.

Sir got out his phone again. "I'll call your parents, and then inform Unc that Hope may need to stay an additional day or two."

"Could you get my phone, Sir? I'd like to call Rytsar back."

He got the phone out of her purse and handed it to her, explaining, "While I'm making those calls, I'll also check the front desk to see if my keys made it back safely."

As she took the phone from him, she squeezed his hand. "Thank you for getting me to the hospital so quickly—with a police escort, no less."

He paused for a moment, then glanced at the fetal monitor. "I'm grateful you and the baby are safe."

Despite his calm exterior, Brie knew he'd been equally shaken by the ordeal. Pressing his hand against her cheek, she looked up at him and smiled. "We are, Sir, because of you."

Welcome to the World

The moment Sir left Brie, it felt like the air had been sucked out of the room. She shivered from the chill of it and immediately called Rytsar.

"*Radost moya*, tell me you are well."

"I am." She smiled to herself, touched by his concern. "In fact, I got the epidural and I'm listening to the baby's heartbeat right now."

She held out the phone so he could hear it, then put the phone back to her ear. "Isn't that a wonderful sound?"

"It is," he answered gruffly.

"I'm sorry we had to cut you off before."

"Although I understand, this is not easy for me."

"I know… Sir's calling my parents and his uncle right now since none of us were prepared for this early arrival."

"What is it with your babes, *radost moya*? Don't they know how good they have it inside your belly?"

She laughed. "I guess they're just eager to meet their *dyadya*."

"I want to be there for the birth." She could hear the sorrow in his voice. "I failed to appreciate how hard the distance would be…" He suddenly changed his tone and asked, "Tell me, how is *moye solntse?*"

"Luckily, she was staying with the Reynolds overnight and wasn't exposed to the chaos this morning." Caressing her stomach, Brie confessed, "I'm trying to be brave."

"I know Kylie's death haunts you today."

"It's so hard not to think of her," she whimpered.

"Take my advice, *radost moya.* Do not dwell on the tragedy. It will only deplete your strength, and it does not honor Kylie's life."

She closed her eyes, soaking in his words. She knew they came from a heart that had suffered unspeakable loss—but had survived.

"You are strong. Say it," he insisted.

"I am strong."

"Today you meet your babe."

"Yes!" Her heart started to race as that feeling of excitement she'd felt earlier today returned. "Do you think the baby is going to be a girl or a boy?"

He chuckled. "I am certain of the sex, but do not wish to spoil it for you."

"Well, you do have a fifty/fifty shot."

"*Nyet.* I know with the same certainty I did with *moye solntse.*"

Brie giggled. "It's easy to make that claim if you're not willing to commit."

"I will prove it to you."

She grinned into the phone. "How?"

"You must have patience, *radost moya.*"

Brie laughed, assuring him, "I promise I won't rub it in if you are wrong."

"And I promise to lick you with my cat o' nines for doubting me."

"I didn't agree to that!" she squeaked.

His sadistic chuckle filled her ears.

Dr. Glas walked into the room and smiled at her. "How are you feeling after the epidural, Mrs. Davis?"

As soon as Rytsar heard the doctor's voice, he commanded, "Tell the good doctor I know the sex of the baby."

Brie snickered. "I'm not going to tell him that."

"Tell him," he insisted.

"Tell me what?" Dr. Glas asked as he glanced over the readings for the fetal monitor.

"Rytsar claims he knows the sex of the baby."

"Is that your friend who attended the last birth?"

"Yes." Brie blushed as she answered, unsure if Dr. Glas understood the true nature of their relationship.

"May I?" he asked, pointing to her phone.

Brie nodded eagerly and handed it to him.

"Okay, I'll bite. What's your guess about the sex?" Dr. Glas asked him. "Okay, I stand corrected…it's not a guess." He winked at Brie.

She smirked, finding it hilarious that Rytsar was correcting her doctor.

"And that's your final answer? Fine, I'll let her know when the time comes."

Dr. Glas handed the phone back to Brie, shaking his head in amusement before telling her, "I need to check your progress, lass."

Before she could speak, Rytsar stated, "Allow the

doctor to do his work," and hung up.

She set the phone down, feeling a little sad that they hadn't been able to finish a conversation with him yet.

After Dr. Glas had examined her, he informed her, "You're continuing to progress, and the babe's oxygen levels remain good."

"That's wonderful news."

"It is, but you may want to tell your Russian friend to hurry. You're progressing faster than the first time."

Brie felt an ache in her heart at the mention of Rytsar. "He's in Russia on important business."

Dr. Glas looked at her thoughtfully. "Well, if you'd like him to be with you during the delivery, I'll give your husband permission to video chat during the birth. I remember how devastated your Russian friend was about missing your daughter's birth…and these are unusual circumstances."

She suspected he was talking about Kylie's recent death and knew Dr. Glas's offer was unusual for the hospital. To Brie, it showed his level of confidence in this delivery, despite the nuchal cord and premature labor. That bolstered her spirits more than he could know.

"It would mean the world to all three of us."

Dr. Glas grinned. "Then make it so, lass."

His compassion touched her deeply.

"Dr. Glas, although it's painful to talk about, I know you did everything you could for Kylie. It's the reason I don't want anyone else delivering my baby."

He said nothing, staring at her for a moment before nodding. "I appreciate your confidence, Mrs. Davis."

Brie glanced at the door and smiled when she saw Sir

walking in.

"What did I miss?"

Dr. Glas cleared his throat before answering Sir. "The baby's oxygen levels are good, and your wife is currently at four centimeters."

"Then she's progressing faster than last time," Sir stated, sounding concerned.

"True, but it's not uncommon for a second birth," Dr. Glas assured him.

Sir nodded, then glanced at Brie. "Your parents are on their way, babygirl."

"Wonderful." Brie smiled at the doctor before telling Sir, "Dr. Glas says we can video chat with Rytsar during the delivery."

Sir turned to Dr. Glas and held out his hand, shaking it firmly. "That is unexpected. Thank you."

He smiled as he returned Sir's handshake. "Certainly, Mr. Davis."

After Dr. Glas left the room to continue his rounds, Brie confessed to Sir, "For the first time since my water broke, I'm starting to feel excited." She looked down at her belly. "We are about to meet you, little one."

Sir laid his hand on her stomach, looking at Brie tenderly. "You are a marvel."

When she shook her head, he stated, "I'm serious, Brie. Your eternal optimism underscores your inner strength."

She blushed under his high praise. "I love you, Sir."

"And I love you," he said, leaning down to kiss her.

She felt pleasant chills the moment their lips touched. His phone started ringing, but Sir refused to break the kiss, kissing her even deeper. Brie sighed in contentment when he finally pulled away.

He quickly glanced at his phone. "It can wait," he told her as he slipped it back in his pocket.

"I've been dying to ask if your car keys were at the front desk."

Sir smiled. "They were, along with a note of congratulations."

"That was kind of a stranger to offer to help us like that."

"It certainly was," he chuckled. "Although I momentarily questioned his intentions at the time."

"I did, too!" Brie laughed. "Let's call Rytsar and tell him the good news about getting permission to video chat with him during the birth. I had to cut our conversation short again because Dr. Glas walked in."

"Good idea," Sir agreed.

Brie could hear the relief in Rytsar's voice when Sir told him he would get to watch the birth. "I am a fortunate man," the Russian stated multiple times during the call.

It thrilled Brie that he would still be a part of the birth.

The moment Brie's parents walked into the room, she could feel the heavy burden of their concern.

Her mother walked up to the bed, carrying a gigantic purse. She handed it to Brie's father, who grunted under the weight of it.

"Oh, honey…" she cried as she hugged Brie tightly.

Her dad leaned over the bed with tears in his eyes and patted her shoulder awkwardly. "It's going to be okay, little girl. We're here now."

She looked at them both and smiled. "Everything is fine," she assured them. "Yes, the baby is coming early—but Hope did, too." She glanced at the monitor. "And the baby is doing great."

Her father swiped the tears from his eye and grumbled, "Of course. Just natural to be concerned like any parent would be."

Her mother grasped Brie's hand and squeezed it before grabbing the giant purse from her husband. "I've had this bag ready for a month. Ever since we learned you were having another baby, I started adding to it."

Brie stared at the huge bag and giggled at her mom. "What do you have in there, the kitchen sink?"

Her mother winked at her. "It's everything you could possibly want during delivery." She started fishing things out one by one. "Magazines to pass the time, some Mad Libs, crossword puzzles—"

"Mom, I don't like crossword puzzles."

"Oh, those are for your father," she stated, handing them to him.

Her mom surprised her by pulling out a portable CD player. "Got some of your favorite music, too."

Brie giggled when her mother placed several old CDs on the bed. "Mom, I haven't listened to this stuff since I was a kid." But then she grabbed one. "Oh…I love Green Day!"

"See, I know you better than you think, sweetheart."

She pulled out individual applesauce and gelatin cups next and explained, "These are to keep your energy up."

Then she fished out a beautiful sea-green robe and laid it out on the bed.

"Oh, Mom. It's so pretty!"

"I thought you might like to wear it for your photos after the baby is born." She patted Brie's hand. "No reason Mommy can't be pampered."

Brie stared at all of the items scattered on the bed. "You've thought of everything."

Her mom hugged her again. "I tried, sweetheart. I just want you to be as comfortable and happy as I can make you today."

Her dad flipped through one of the crosswords and asked Sir, "How are you holding up, son?"

Sir looked at him with cautious optimism. "Better now."

"This whole birthing thing is rough on a man," her father stated solemnly.

"I'm fine, Daddy," Brie reminded him.

"You have no idea what it's like being your father, young lady."

She looked at him in surprise. "What do you mean?"

He frowned at her. "You always test my limits."

Brie giggled. "You act as if I'm your Domme."

Her father stared at her, the expression on his face so comical that she burst out laughing.

Before he could take offense, Sir clapped him on the back. "Why don't we get the ladies some hot tea?"

After they left the room, her mother scolded Brie. "You really shouldn't tease your father like that."

"But, Mom…"

When her mother met her gaze, Brie stopped mid-sentence, realizing how upset she was. "Brianna, how would you feel if you heard Hope was being rushed to the hospital? After everything that's happened, your father has been beside himself. Give him a little grace, sweetheart. He loves you more than you know."

"I know that, Mom. He just…has a rough way of showing it."

"I'll admit he's not sophisticated like Thane, but his heart is just as big."

"It is," Brie agreed.

Her mother gave her a crooked smile. "But I will never forget the look on his face just now. It was priceless…"

"I wish I'd had my camera out."

They both started giggling.

When the men returned Brie was properly humble to her father and all was forgiven.

The next few hours pass by pleasantly. Then the contractions started getting more intense and lasting longer.

Luckily for Brie, the epidural made it painless. She could feel when the contractions were happening, but they didn't hurt at all.

"I love epidurals," she murmured happily.

Sir chuckled. "I must admit that this is a completely different experience from the first time."

Brie smiled at him, then turned to her mother. "I'm sorry you didn't get the chance to experience how awesome epidurals are."

Her mom laughed. "Oh, Lord, there wasn't time. One minute, I'm telling Bill we need to get to the hospital, and the next, I'm screaming, 'The baby's coming, the baby's coming!' as we pull up to the emergency room."

Her father shook his head. "I almost had a heart attack on the drive there."

"I'm sure my husband can relate," Brie told her dad, gazing lovingly at Sir.

Her dad slapped him on the back. "You got her here safely and that's the only thing that matters. Am I right?"

"Agreed," Sir replied with a half-smile.

Dr. Glas walked into the room and asked her parents to leave so he could check her. "I see the contractions remain steady and strong. Let's see how far you've progressed," he stated, positioning himself between her legs.

Brie watched his expression with interest.

"It's official. You're fully dilated, lass."

He glanced at Sir, "You may want to give your Russian friend a call. It won't be long now."

Dr. Glas asked Brie, "Are you ready to find out the sex of your child?"

Brie felt butterflies when she answered, "Never been more ready!"

While the doctor left to gather the team, her parents filed back in. "I'm going to wait in the waiting room," her father announced, leaning down to kiss Brie on the forehead.

He grabbed the stack of crosswords and said, "I love you, little girl," before quickly exiting the room.

Her mother watched him go and sighed. "I'm afraid he's not any good seeing people he loves in pain."

"Understandable," Sir replied.

Brie took Sir's hand and gazed up at him. "Lucky for me, Sir has no issues with that."

He winked at her, acknowledging the double meaning.

"I'm sorry, sweetheart, but I have to join him. Bill is trying hard to cover it, but he's a mess."

"I understand, Mom."

She hugged Brie hard before turning to Sir, but she wasn't quick enough and Brie caught the worried look she gave Sir.

"Let me walk you out, Mrs. Bennett," Sir replied, escorting her out of the room.

When he returned a few minutes later, Brie asked him, "What was that all about?"

"Your parents are concerned about your well-being, babygirl. They just needed some reassurance."

Brie could understand why they were worried, but she no longer had any doubts that both she and the baby would be fine. It allowed her to savor this moment without any fear.

"I'm calling Durov," Sir informed her, holding the phone so Brie could see Rytsar when he answered.

"*Radost moya*!" Rytsar bellowed when the phones connected.

"Rytsar!" she cried back. "Are you ready to become a *dyadya* again?"

He stared at her with those intense blue eyes and stated, "It is my greatest honor."

Brie felt tingles in her soul knowing he meant it. "I'm grateful you can be here with us."

"While it is not the same as being there in person, this will do."

Sir smiled at him. "I agree, old friend."

"How are you holding up, Brother?"

Sir glanced at Brie. "Better than expected, considering the start to the day."

"Actually, it started out perfect," she told Rytsar. "It wasn't until I started drinking Nonna's hot chocolate that everything went south…"

Two nurses walked in behind Dr. Glas. He smiled confidently at Brie and clapped his hands together. "Let's deliver this babe."

The nurses moved to either side of Brie to help support her legs during delivery while Sir stood beside Brie with one hand on her shoulder as he continued their video call with Rytsar.

When Dr. Glas told Brie to bear down, she felt an inner confidence she had never felt before and pushed for all she was worth. After the powerful contraction passed, she looked up at Sir and the camera with eager anticipation.

"Keep pushing until I tell you to stop," Dr. Glas instructed her when the next contraction hit. "Puuussshhh!"

The two nurses pressed her legs toward her chest, giving Brie more leverage. She took advantage of it and was able to push even harder. Brie suddenly heard the baby's heart rate drop and turned her head toward the monitor in concern.

Dr. Glas ordered her in a calm voice to stop pushing. "There's no need to worry. The baby is far enough down that I should be able to work on the cord."

Brie lay completely still while Dr. Glas worked to loosen the cord around their baby's neck. Because of the epidural, she only felt the pressure of his hands inside her. Everyone in the room remained silent as the doctor concentrated on manipulating the cord.

Brie closed her eyes she listened to the baby's heart rate continue to beat erratically. When it finally returned to normal, she heard a collective sigh of relief from Sir and Rytsar.

Dr. Glas looked up from between Brie's legs and smiled. "I want you to be ready to push hard with the next contraction."

Brie nodded. Putting everything she had into it, she screamed from sheer effort when she started pushing.

After several minutes, Dr. Glas advised her, "Give yourself a few deep breaths, lass, and we'll start again."

Brie nodded and lay back on the bed, panting heavily.

"You're doing great, *radost moya*. Such power!"

She turned her head and smiled at him.

Sir swept away the strands of sweaty hair clinging to her face. "You are the essence of feminine power, téa."

Strengthened by Sir's praise, she nodded to the doctor to signal she was ready. Brie braced herself. As soon as he told her to push, she growled fiercely as she powered through it.

She was soon rewarded when she heard Rytsar cry out excitedly, "I see the head! I see the head!"

A cry of victory escaped Brie's lips as the pressure increased and the baby's head was forced out.

"Wait for the next contraction," Dr. Glas ordered.

Brie lay back, grateful for the momentary rest.

"This is incredible, *moy droog!*" she heard Rytsar yell at Sir.

"It is," he agreed as he smiled down at Brie.

Sir squeezed Brie's hand firmly. "This is it, babygirl. Just one more push."

She smiled up at him, feeling like a goddamn power-house!

Taking a deep breath, she braced herself again when the next contraction hit.

"We just need to get the shoulders out and you're done."

With a herculean effort she pushed again, gritting her teeth. Suddenly, the intense pressure disappeared as the baby's shoulders slipped through.

"Congratulations, Mrs. Davis." Dr. Glas held up their crying baby and grinned. "Your Russian friend is right. You are the mother to a fine son." He laid the tiny infant on her chest and the baby immediately quieted.

Brie stared down at her son in awe. "Is he healthy, Dr. Glas?"

"He may be small, but as you can tell from his bois-terous entrance, he appears to be quite healthy."

"Our little boy…" Brie murmured, caressing his cheek.

Sir leaned down to kiss her. "Another miracle."

She lifted her head to meet his kiss. "I love making babies with you."

Brie then glanced at Rytsar. "You were right, *dyadya*. We have a son."

He nodded. "*Da*, you do."

Grinning, Rytsar addressed Sir. "Congratulations, Brother. Are you ready to make number three?"

Sir gave him the side-eye. "We're not having five children, old friend."

Dr. Glas interrupted them. "Mr. Davis, would you like to cut the cord?"

"Yes, I would."

"It's time to let me go, *moy droog,*" Rytsar stated hastily. "But, before you do, I must know the name of my *plemyannik.*"

Sir nodded to Brie, wanting her to share it.

Brie smiled at Rytsar. "Naturally, his middle name is Alonzo, in honor of Sir's father. And, to honor my side of the family, we chose to name him after my father's favorite grandfather." She smiled at him when she added, "The name is also a nod to you."

Glancing down at their tiny son, Brie made the formal introduction. "Rytsar, I would like you to meet Anthony Alonzo Davis."

The proud grin on his face when she looked up at Rytsar touched Brie deeply.

"That is a strong name appropriate for a Davis," he stated. Before he hung up, however, Rytsar spoke to Brie in Russian. "*Slova ne opisat' moyu lyubov' k tebe.*"

Words cannot describe my love for you...

Brie smiled and blew him a kiss with tears in her eyes.

After putting the phone back in his pocket, Sir took the surgical scissors from Dr. Glas. The moment he cut the umbilical cord, Brie realized that the tiny human she had carried for almost nine months was now independent of her.

She looked down at their little boy, her heart bursting with love.

We have a son...

Tears of Joy

B rie watched with apprehension as the neonatal nurse left with their newborn to perform a thorough examination.

"No need to worry, Mrs. Davis," Dr. Glas assured her. "Your son's vitals are good."

Brie smiled at him wearily. "Why did both babies come so early?"

He shook his head. "It may be coincidence or it's simply your normal gestation period."

"Whatever the case, we are profoundly grateful to you, Dr. Glas," Sir stated, holding out his hand. "You were able to bring our son safely into the world despite the complications."

Dr. Glas shook Sir's hand warmly. "Given the circumstances, I appreciate the trust you both placed in me."

Even though the memory was painful, Brie told him, "I will never forget seeing you at Kylie's funeral, Dr. Glas. It showed how much you truly care."

The doctor let out a ragged sigh. "Her unexpected

death was an unfortunate tragedy, but I trust their babe is doing well."

Brie smiled, choosing not to mention Faelan. "Yes, the entire community has rallied together to help. It's been a beautiful thing to witness."

He grinned. "That's good to hear."

A nurse popped her head into the room. "Dr. Glas, Mrs. Clancy is about to deliver in room 408."

Dr. Glas nodded to the nurse. "Thank you, Trudy."

He turned back to Brie. "Excuse me. Duty calls."

"Please, go assist in another miracle," she told him.

After he left, Sir lowered the railing to hug Brie. "Your strength and determination today were a sight to behold, babygirl."

"I would have done anything to protect our baby." She then whispered in his ear, "Just like you."

When Sir pulled away, she noticed a tear in his eye. After the terrifying start to the day, they both understood how lucky they were.

"I'll go get your parents. I'm sure they are anxious to see you."

"Before you go, Sir, can you help me into the robe?" Brie asked him.

"Certainly, babygirl."

Sir helped her slip into the robe and adjusted the collar before cinching her tie. "Beautiful…" he murmured, kissing her on the lips before he left.

Looking around the empty room, Brie immediately thought of Kylie. Instead of fear and sadness, she was blessed by a vision of Kylie smiling as she held her little girl. Brie was overcome with joy as if Kylie was in the room, celebrating this moment with her.

You are not forgotten, Kylie…

"Oh, Brie!" her mother cried, rushing into the room. "How are you doing, sweetheart?"

Brie turned to her, smiling. "We have a beautiful baby boy, Mom."

Her father strode into the room. "I'm proud of you, Brianna. I didn't want to let on, but I was worried about you, young lady. But look at you now! You're positively glowing—and the baby is doing well?"

Brie gratefully accepted her father's hug. "He's doing great, Daddy."

"Thane told us he came out hollering."

Brie giggled. "Yes, he certainly did."

"That's always a good sign." He patted her on the head like he did when she was a little girl. "Because you did, too."

"I did?"

"Yes, your screams could be heard throughout the maternity ward."

Brie blushed and glanced at Sir. She could tell by his sexy smirk that he was remembering her desperate screams of "I'm not a masochist!"

Her mother started fishing in her large purse and pulled out a wrapped gift with a blue bow.

"What's this? You already got me this beautiful robe."

"I brought something for the baby."

Brie carefully opened the package to find a soft, knitted blanket of sky blue. "How did you know it would be a boy?" she asked in surprise.

Her mother laughed. "I didn't." She proceeded to pull out another package wrapped with a pink bow.

Brie held up the blanket in admiration. "I love it, but I love even more that you made two of them."

Her mother grinned. "I just wanted your child to know how much he is loved."

Brie's bottom lip trembled. She felt completely overwhelmed with happiness. "I love you, Mom."

The neonatal nurse walked into the room, holding their crying son. Both of her parents "oohed" and "aahed" while the nurse placed him in Brie's open arms. "He is in perfect health but is missing his mother," she explained.

As Brie tried to comfort him, the nurse asked gently, "Would you like me to bring in the lactation nurse?"

She looked up and shook her head. "No, we'll be okay."

Brie then glanced at her father. "Are you comfortable staying while I feed him, Daddy?"

In the past, her father had been squeamish about it whenever she'd breastfed Hope.

Sucking in his breath, he let it out slowly before answering. "It's completely natural. No reason I should feel uncomfortable." He sounded as if he was trying to convince himself, but Brie took him at his word and loosened the ties of her robe so she could breastfeed her baby for the first time.

The moment her son felt the warmth of her skin against his cheek, he instantly quieted and turned his head, seeking his mother's milk. With a little guidance, Brie helped him to latch on and he began sucking hungrily.

"Poor thing was starving," Brie murmured with compassion.

She looked up at Sir. "Maybe that's why he came out crying."

The nurse smiled. "Congratulations Mr. and Mrs. Davis. If you need anything or have any questions, please feel free to ring one of the nurses."

After she left, Brie turned her focus back on her son. She'd had no idea that she could love another human being as much as she loved Hope.

"My precious little boy…"

She gazed down at him tenderly, marveling at this perfect child in her arms. Anthony shared the same olive skin as his sister, but unlike Hope, the shape of his nose and lips were strikingly similar to Sir's.

"You're so handsome," she cooed, kissing his soft baby head.

Once he was full, Anthony quickly fell asleep. Knowing Sir hadn't had the chance to hold him yet, she carefully held him out to Sir. "Meet your son, Papa."

Sir cradled him in his arms and smiled. "Welcome to the world, my son."

Brie felt a tingling sensation run up her spine as a vision of Alonzo came to her mind. She could imagine Alonzo doing the same thing when Sir was born. It was as if life was coming full circle.

"I must say, you do make handsome children," her father told Brie, looking at their son. "I can definitely see the Bennett in him."

Although Brie couldn't see it, she agreed. "Yes! He's the best of both families—just like Hope."

Her mother made cooing noises as she stroked his cheek with her finger. "I think it's lovely that the two of you chose to name the baby after Bill's grandfather."

Bill nodded, stating proudly, "It was an unexpected honor."

Brie smiled at her dad. "It was important to us that both families were represented, and I've never forgotten all of the stories you shared about your grandpa, Daddy."

Her father's voice was ripe with emotion when he told Thane, "I've never met a better man than Grandpop. He never complained, worked hard all his life, and always had a piece of candy in his pocket for his grandchildren." He chuckled, then suddenly cleared his throat, overwhelmed with emotion. "I loved that man…"

"I barely remember Pop-Pop," Brie admitted, "but I do remember the candy."

"I was glad he had the chance to meet you, Brianna. It was important to me." He glanced at her son, brimming with pride. "Mark my words, young lady. Anthony is going to be a leader among men."

Brie was deeply touched by her father's words. For a man who was guarded about his feelings—this was unexpected. It seemed being here for the birth had changed something in him.

Sir passed their son on to Brie's mother. "I would like to call Nonna."

"Yes, I would love that!" Brie agreed, feeling a tug at her heart thinking about Sir's grandparents.

He dialed the number and winked at Brie when he said, "Nonna, our son came a little early."

Brie could hear the old woman's delighted cry.

Sir's eyes sparkled with joy when he told her, "Yes, a healthy baby boy."

Brie could hear Nonna's muffled voice as she repeated everything Sir said to Nonno. The excitement Brie heard in her voice was heartwarming.

"His name is Anthony Alonzo Davis."

The phone suddenly became silent, and Brie looked at Sir in concern.

"There's no need to cry, Nonna," Sir said soothingly, but the sweet old woman could not seem to stop crying.

Finally, Sir handed the phone to Brie, telling Nonna, "Brianna would love to talk to you."

Brie pressed his cell phone against her cheek and spoke in Italian. "It's okay, Nonna…"

"I'm just so happy!" Nonna sobbed. "The tears won't stop, Nipotina."

Brie understood her immense joy, so rather than trying to make the tears stop, she said, "He looks like Thane. You won't believe the resemblance."

"I…I…" Nonna sobbed several more times before handing the phone to her husband.

Nonno apologized. "Forgive her, Nipotina. She's overcome with joy."

"No need for apologies, Nonno. Happy tears are a gift."

"Will you be coming to visit soon?" he asked hopefully.

Brie covered the phone with her hand and told Sir, "They're wondering when we're coming to visit."

He chuckled. "Our son is not even a few hours old and they already want us to fly across the ocean to visit?"

"It's so sweet," Brie giggled.

Brie's dad suddenly spoke up. "Take it for what it's worth, Thane. We never know what the future will bring."

Sir nodded thoughtfully. "I appreciate the advice, Dad."

Looking to Brie, Sir asked, "How do you feel?"

She answered truthfully. "When I think of Nonna holding our son, I can't get there soon enough."

Sir smiled. "Then tell Nonno that we'll make the trip when it is safe for both mother and child."

Brie loved being the one to give them the happy news and laughed with joy when poor Nonna burst out in a fresh set of tears.

She handed the phone back to Sir. "You've just made your *nonna* the happiest woman on the planet."

"Not me, my dear. This is all you."

Sir finished the conversation, filling the hospital room with the beautiful lilt of the Italian language.

There is one thing missing... Brie thought.

After Sir hung up, Brie's dad surprised them both by stating, "In no way am I trying to sound ungrateful for your choice in naming your son after my grandfather, but I have to admit I'm surprised you didn't give him the first name Alonzo." He glanced at his wife. "We both know how much you loved your father, Thane."

Sir glanced at Brie. "We talked it over extensively. You're right. I loved my father deeply. However, I don't want our son living in his shadow. I know my father would feel the same. Anthony will be free to make his way in the world without any expectations beyond his own talents and desires."

Brie's dad gave him a look of admiration. "You are a very wise man, Thane. Much wiser than your years."

Brie put her hand over her mouth to hide her smile. She knew how much the word "wise" grated on Sir's nerves but he didn't even bat an eye. "Thank you."

Slapping Sir on the back, her dad told him, "Well, I'd better get Marcy home. It's been quite an eventful day for all of us!"

"It meant so much that you were able to share this moment with me," Brie said as she hugged her parents.

"It will go down as one of the greatest days of my life, Brianna," her dad answered.

Brie hugged him again with tears in her eyes.

Her mother couldn't resist giving her one last peck on the cheek before she left. "The best decision we ever made was moving to California so we didn't miss this."

After they left, Brie let out a long sigh.

"What's wrong, babygirl?"

She looked up at him and confessed, "I miss Hope."

"You're in luck," he said with a wink. "Unc should be here shortly."

"Really?"

"I've missed our little girl, too," he admitted, laying Anthony back in her arms. "Our family doesn't feel complete without Hope."

Brie cuddled Anthony against her, murmuring happily, "I couldn't agree more, Sir."

Complete

"Sweet pea!" Brie cried, thrilled beyond words to see her daughter when Mr. Reynolds carried Hope into the hospital room.

As soon as Hope saw her mother, her entire face lit up and she struggled in Mr. Reynold's arms, wanting to get down.

"She definitely missed her mama," he laughed, quickly walking to the bed.

Brie grabbed Hope in a hug, kissing her all over. "Oh, how Mommy missed you!"

Hope giggled and then suddenly stopped when she saw Sir holding the baby. She pointed at him and started bouncing excitedly.

Sir brought Anthony over, leaning in so Hope could get her first look at her brother. "Little angel, you have a baby brother to look after now," he told her.

Hope stared at the baby in silence, then looked at Brie.

"That's your little brother Anthony," Brie said encouragingly, pronouncing his name slowly for her.

"An-ta-nee?"

Brie nodded. When Hope reached out to touch his cheek, Brie held her breath. Anthony stared transfixed at his sister as if he already knew her.

It was such a sweet moment, it made Brie teary. When she looked up and saw Sir's tender smile, it completely stole her breath away.

This is the most beautiful moment of my life…

Mr. Reynolds stood back, looking at them with an expression of profound love. Here was the man who had taken on the role of caregiver to Sir all those years ago. By Sir's own admission, he had not been an easy child to live with after his father died, but Mr. Reynolds remained patient and loved Thane throughout those difficult years.

Mr. Reynolds had also hired Brie after she'd graduated from college, when she was in desperate need of a job to cover her rent. It was in that tiny tobacco shop that she'd first met Sir.

In a true sense, Mr. Reynolds helped create the family they were now.

"Thank you," Brie told him with a full heart.

He smiled, shaking his head. "No need to thank me. I was happy to come as soon as Thane called. Hope shouldn't miss this chance to meet her little brother."

"I don't mean just that. You have done so much for me all these years…" Brie was suddenly so overcome with emotion she choked on the rest of her words.

"There, there," Mr. Reynolds said gently. "No reason to cry on my account."

"Brie's right," Sir replied. "We owe you a great deal, Unc."

Mr. Reynold's chuckled lightly. "You're wrong there,

Thane. It has been my honor to be a part of your life. To see how far you have come is truly inspiring. This is the family *you* created."

"Because of your unfailing love," Sir answered, his voice clear but tinged with emotion.

Mr. Reynolds nodded humbly, accepting their praise.

"Would you like to hold him, Unc?"

It was a solemn moment when Sir placed his son in his uncle's arms. However, it was soon broken by Hope's excited chatter as she bounced on Brie's chest while reaching for the baby.

Sir rescued Brie by quickly sweeping Hope into his arms. "It seems our little girl can't get enough of her baby brother."

Watching the four of them together, Brie felt the urge to take a picture with her phone. She gazed at the sight wistfully, realizing that all four of them were connected by the blood of Sir's mother. It was proof that something of remarkable worth had come out of the love that Alonzo and Ruth shared—despite how it all ended.

Knowing that filled Brie with a deep sense of hope for the future.

Mr. Reynolds laid Anthony in her arms, stating, "I'm going to head out for a bit so you can spend time alone together. I'll be back to pick Hope up in a couple of hours."

"You don't have to do that," Brie said, although she loved the idea.

He gave her a kind smile. "This is our gift to you. Judy and I discussed it before I left. We want to give you time as a family."

Brie glanced at Sir, who nodded.

"We gratefully accept," she replied, squeezing his hand tight.

After he left, Anthony started to wiggle in her arms and let out a whimpering cry. Hope pointed to him, clearly distressed.

"It's okay, sweet pea. Your brother is just hungry."

While she fed him, Sir lowered the railing on the other side of the bed and set Hope next to Brie. Grabbing a chair, he sat down and began running his fingers through Brie's hair.

"Oh, that feels good..." she purred, enjoying the tingles his fingers caused. She lay there in silence, enjoying this intimate moment as a family.

While Brie was burping Anthony, Rytsar called. Hope immediately responded when Sir switched the phone to speaker and she heard, "Is all well, *moy droog*?"

"*Dyadya*!"

"Is that my *moye solntse*?"

She crawled over Brie to get to the phone.

"Hope appears eager to talk to you, Brother," Sir laughed when she grabbed at his phone.

Not understanding it was on speaker, she put it up to her ear and started babbling excitedly. Rytsar interjected with comments as if they were having a deep conversation.

Brie smiled at Sir. It was too adorable for words.

When Hope was done talking, she let go of the phone and crawled back over to Brie to snuggle up with her little brother.

"In answer to your question earlier, all is definitely well," Sir told Rytsar.

"And how are you feeling, *radost moya*?"

"Exhausted but happy."

"It's no wonder you are tired," he chuckled. "You have ushered another human into the world."

She sighed in contentment. "Considering how the day started, it couldn't have ended on a sweeter note, including this call right now."

His voice was full of warmth when he told her, "I am about to begin my day knowing the people that I love are well."

"We are," she answered feeling truly grateful.

As if to contradict her, Anthony began to fuss loudly.

"I don't know what's wrong," Brie told Sir when she couldn't comfort him. "I just fed him, and his diaper is dry."

She handed Anthony to Sir, but he had no better luck than she did trying to calm him down.

Hope became upset hearing the baby cry and kept patting Brie, wanting Brie to help her little brother.

"Let me try," Rytsar stated. The deep tenor of his voice suddenly filled the room with his presence as he sang his mother's lullaby.

Instantly, Anthony quieted as he stared in the direction of his voice.

Rytsar sang the song several times. Brie looked at Hope and smiled, noticing she was struggling to keep her eyes open. By the time he was finished, both children were fast asleep.

Brie whispered, "Your voice has worked its magic."

"I can tell you've kept your promise, *radost moya*," he stated proudly.

"Yes, they hear your voice every night before bed,"

she assured him.

"I am pleased."

The three spoke quietly while the children slept. Sir continued to play with Brie's hair, and it wasn't long before her own eyelids grew heavy.

Brie tried to fight it off, but exhaustion overwhelmed her as she listened to the soothing voices of both men.

"Complete," she murmured.

"What was that?" Sir asked, interrupting his conversation with Rytsar.

She turned her head toward him with a sleepy smile. "It feels complete."

"Yes, it does, babygirl," he whispered, kissing her gently.

The next morning, Brie's parents came to keep Brie company while Sir drove the Lotus home to pick up the family car.

Brie thought nothing of it and enjoyed the time alone with her parents, especially her father. There was a greater ease between them now than existed in years past. Brie had always been good friends with her mother growing up, but her father had held certain expectations of Brie that she never seemed to meet.

His lofty expectations left her feeling like she never measured up and that caused tension between them. But things were starting to change…

Brie wasn't sure if it was because her father was getting mellower with age, or if he had finally come to accept the path she'd chosen. Regardless, she felt closer to her dad in this moment than she had her entire life.

When it finally came time for her to be discharged, Dr. Glas insisted on personally escorting her out of the hospital. As he pushed the wheelchair toward their car, he said with a lopsided grin, "It has been a pleasure, Mrs. Davis."

Brie smiled up at him. "I will forever be grateful to you, Dr. Glas." Glancing at her son wrapped in the blue, knitted blanket, she added, "And I will always remember this delivery with fondness."

"As will I, Mrs. Davis."

He then shook Sir's hand firmly. "If you should need my services in the future, please don't hesitate to call."

Sir chuckled. "I'm certain that won't be necessary but thank you."

Brie sighed as they pulled away from the hospital. She couldn't help thinking of Kylie and Faelan. Neither of them got to experience this moment of leaving together with their baby girl.

It was heartbreaking.

Brie glanced up at the sky, overwhelmed with sadness for Faelan.

Sir reached out to take her hand. "Is something wrong, babygirl?"

"Faelan…" she choked out.

"We will see him through the wilderness," he stated with conviction.

Brie nodded, trusting that they would.

He squeezed her hand reassuringly. "It is important to concentrate your energy on yourself and the children for now, so you will be strong enough to help him when the time comes."

"That is…" She almost said "wise", but thankfully caught herself in time. "…exactly what I will do, Sir."

"Good."

The drive home was nothing like the drive to the hospital. Sir drove to the beach at a leisurely pace to make sure her parents kept up with them in their own car.

Once they arrived home, Brie was surprised to see a number of vehicles parked at the house. "What's going on?"

Sir smirked. "Rather than feign ignorance, I'll tell you the truth. Ms. Taylor refused to cancel your baby shower."

Brie laughed. "Oh, my goodness. That was supposed to be today, wasn't it?" She looked back at Anthony and smiled. "You little troublemaker."

"I told them to keep it short so you can rest, but I thought you might enjoy a small gathering."

Brie recognized the Reynolds' van and Lea's beat-up car, as well as Mary's fancy new wheels. "This is exactly what my heart needed, Sir."

He helped her out of the car before getting Anthony from the car seat. As they walked up to the door, he said, "You can choose to act surprised or not. It's totally up to you, babygirl."

The door swung open before they even reached the porch.

Lea cried, "It's Stinky Cheese and her littlest Brie!"

Giggling, Brie hugged Lea tightly, then noticed Mary standing behind her.

"It's good to see you, Mary."

She shrugged. "Whatever…"

"No, I'm serious," Brie insisted, releasing Lea to hug Mary.

The girl was stiff in her arms, but whispered, "Good to see you too, Stinks." Brie gave her an extra squeeze before letting go.

Brie immediately bent down to catch Hope, who came barreling toward her excitedly. Lifting her up, Brie cuddled Hope against her, telling the Reynolds, "You wouldn't think she saw me last night, would you?"

"It's the way of little girls," Brie's mother said, walking up to her. "Hope will always need her mommy no matter how old she gets."

Brie smiled at her mom before turning back to Judy. "I want to thank you for watching Hope for us, and for last night's gift."

"The truth is we love watching these two play together, Brianna. It's purely selfish on our part." Judy coxed little Jonathan to say hi to her, but he was suddenly overcome with shyness and hid behind her legs.

Judy glanced at Anthony in Sir's arms. "It's wonderful that Jonathan has another cousin to play with."

"Do you want to see, Anthony?" Brie asked Jonathan.

He just looked up at her with wide eyes.

Brie handed Hope to her mother and took Anthony from Sir. Walking to the couch, she sat down and unwrapped Anthony from the blanket so Jonathan could get a better look at him.

But Jonathan remained where he was until Brie's mother put Hope down and she toddled toward her little brother. It seemed to break Jonathan of his shyness, and he quickly raced over to join Hope.

It wasn't until then that Brie noticed Candy hanging up the last of the baby shower decorations. When Lea saw the direction of Brie's gaze, she cried, "Surprise! It's your second After Baby Baby Shower."

"Oh, my goodness, you guys," Brie squealed in mock surprise. "You shouldn't have!"

Lea gave Mary a hip bump. "See, I told you she'd love it."

Mary rolled her eyes, but Brie could see a glint of satisfaction on her face. "I don't know *why* you insist on having your babies before the baby showers, Stinks."

Brie laughed. "Don't blame me. It's these little munchkins."

"Well, I for one am happy to get a closer look at your little alien," Lea cooed, walking over with Candy to ogle the baby. "They're so much cuter outside the stomach."

Brie shook her head, laughing at Lea.

"So, we're sparing you the lame-ass games this time, since time is limited," Mary informed her, rolling her eyes at Lea.

"But, if you want one, I've got it in my car," Lea piped up. "The game involves diapers and chocolate candy bars."

Brie groaned at the thought, "I'll pass."

Candy giggled. "I remember how Lea creamed us with the clothespin game."

"Oh, I love that game!" Brie's mother piped up.

"Thankfully, today it's just about stuffing Brie's de-flated belly with food," Mary stated, pointing to the kitchen counter laden with finger foods. "Got any preferences, Stinks?"

Brie was about to stand up when her father stopped her. "You just tell me what you want, little girl, and I'll get it for you."

Brie looked up at her dad in surprise. "I…well, I'd like a little of everything."

"You got it," he answered, heading to the kitchen.

She glanced at her mother in astonishment. Her dad had never served her before in his entire life.

When the doorbell rang, Sir offered to answer it. "Brie, you may want to see this," he called out after opening the door.

Brie stood up with Anthony cradled in her arms and walked toward the foyer. The moment she saw who was in the doorway, her heart skipped a beat.

"Tono!"

She couldn't believe he was standing there in the flesh beside Autumn.

Brie ran to him and, without thinking, pressed her head against his chest. She closed her eyes, needing to hear his heartbeat. Tears ran down her cheeks as she listened to the strength of each beat.

Suddenly realizing that Sir was the only other person in the room, besides Autumn, who knew about Tono's health scare, she quickly pulled away. To cover up her emotional outburst, Brie wiped her eyes with one hand and muttered, "I'm sorry. Must be the hormones. It's just so good to see you two."

She took Autumn's hand and squeezed it. "I seriously can't believe you're here!"

Autumn grinned at Brie. "Tono insisted I come for your baby shower."

"Little did we know we'd get to meet your son in person." Tono chuckled warmly, looking down at the baby.

Brie's heart burst with joy when she gently placed her son in his arms. "Tono Nosaka, I'm honored to have you to meet our son, Anthony Alonzo Davis."

"The honor is mine." Tono looked down at the child with tenderness.

Autumn stroked Anthony's cheek lightly. "He's so tiny, Brie…"

She laughed. "He's actually bigger than Hope was when she was born."

"It's hard to believe she was ever that small," Autumn remarked, glancing at Hope.

Leaning in, Autumn whispered to Brie, "Thank you for the basket. It meant so much to me."

Brie smiled at Autumn in pleasant shock. "I still can't believe this is real…"

Glancing at Candy, Mary, and Lea, it suddenly dawned on Brie. "Autumn was the only one missing from my first baby shower…"

Lea nodded proudly. "It wouldn't be the same without her, so I sent her an invitation." She squealed excitely. "But I didn't know until yesterday that she was actually coming."

Tono told Brie, "We decided to take a couple of days off so we could make the trip." He looked down at Anthony again. "It was a fortunate choice."

Brie was concerned about Tono's health and asked, "But…what about…" She hesitated. "…the tour?"

Tono understood the nature of her concern and smiled reassuringly. "This trip was important to both of us."

Brie was touched that they'd come, but still worried about him. "I…"

Her father walked up to her carrying two plates piled with food. "I got everything you asked for. Now, sit down and enjoy it before it gets cold."

Brie blushed at the amount of food he had amassed on the plates and was thankful they weren't in Italy where she would feel pressured to eat it all. "Thanks, Daddy."

She whispered to Tono under her breath, "My dad gave me enough for three people…"

He chuckled quietly.

"Everyone needs to fill up their plates," Lea stated, grabbing Autumn's arm. "This is a celebration, people!"

Although it was easy to see how thrilled Lea was to see Autumn, Brie could tell by the expression on Autumn's face that she needed this reunion even more.

Tono handed the baby to Brie's mother, who had been standing beside him, anxious to hold the baby.

"Ren, would you like to join Brie on the couch? I'd be happy to get you anything you like," Sir offered.

"A tall glass of water sounds good."

"I will hear of no such thing, Tono Nosaka!" Lea cried. "You flew Autumn halfway across the world and deserve to be pampered for that."

The moment Tono sat down, Shadow appeared at his feet and let out a low, welcoming meow.

Brie grinned. "Wow, he must have been missing you, too."

Tono bent down to pet the large black cat. "We are two old souls."

Lea came waltzing over to him carrying a plate heaped with food. "I remember all your favorites. I think you'll really like the mini-pizzas I made especially for you," she said with a wink.

As Tono stared at the huge plate, Brie commented, "Looks like you and I have a similar problem."

Knowing Tono couldn't eat anything Lea had dished up because of his restricted diet for his condition, Brie took several items from his plate and plopped them onto hers while no one was looking.

She giggled. "Mine's so ridiculously full, nobody will even notice."

Sir joined them, handing Tono the glass of water.

"Thank you, Sir Davis."

Sir nodded. "I'm glad you could make it."

"How are you feeling?" Brie asked Tono quietly.

He leaned in and told her in a low voice, "I was given clearance to travel. There is no reason for you to worry."

She looked him over with a critical eye. Tono had lost weight, as well as muscle tone, but other than that, he looked like himself even down to the gentle look in his chocolate brown eyes.

"I'm grateful you're here," she confessed, not realizing how much she'd needed to see him face to face.

Tono glanced at Sir. "Thank you again for making the arrangements."

"Think nothing of it, Ren."

Brie tilted her head. "You arranged this, Sir?"

"It was needed."

She stared at him in surprise, completely speechless.

Sir winked at her. "You'd better start eating, my dear.

Your father is eyeing your consumption closely."

Brie obediently picked up one of the mini pizzas from her plate and held it up for her dad to see before shoving it into her mouth and giving him a thumbs up.

Tono watched her with amusement. "Your father seems very attentive toward you."

"Yes," she said after chewing and swallowing. "Things have changed between us lately."

"My heart is glad to hear it."

Even though she knew it was a difficult subject for Tono, she asked him, "How are things with your mother?"

"We continue to speak on a weekly basis."

"But nothing has changed between you?"

"I give her whatever she requires. She wants nothing more from me."

Brie frowned slightly.

"She has given me my freedom," he reminded her gently. He glanced over at Autumn. "It is the greatest gift she is capable of giving, and I am profoundly appreciative of it."

Brie understood that Autumn was in his life because of it. "I hear what you are saying, Tono, but is it wrong that I wish more from your mother?"

Rather than answering, he asked, "Have you heard anything more about the film?"

She shook her head but smiled. "I'm following your advice and have moved on. Actually, I've uncovered something interesting—"

The sound of Anthony's tiny wail suddenly filled the air. Brie immediately excused herself, her breasts aching in response to his cries. Brie retreated to the private patio out back to feed him and was grateful when Mary came to join her.

"You doing okay, Stinks?"

"I should be asking you that," she said, undoing the front of her bra. Anthony immediately latched on and began to suckle.

Mary waved off Brie's concern. "I saw that exchange between you and Tono. What's going on with the rope freak?"

Brie sighed, silently cursing Mary's keen observation skills. "I am…not allowed to discuss it."

"It's his health, isn't it?"

When Brie said nothing, Mary nodded. "Yeah, Lea's oblivious because she's so wrapped up in seeing Autumn again that she failed to question your strange interaction or the physical change in Tono."

"He's fine," Brie insisted.

"Sure he is…"

"So, what's going on with you? I can't handle the radio silence, especially knowing you're with Greg again."

"I'm fine."

Brie realized Mary had chosen to answer her with the same reply Brie had given her about Tono.

Before she could question her on it, however, Mary threw her off by telling her, "I've thought of the perfect name for the new kid." She nodded toward the baby. "Since your nickname is Stinks, you should name this one Little Stinker."

Brie stared at Mary in shock. "Wait! That sounded an awful lot like Lea humor."

"No! Not even close."

Brie raised an eyebrow as she gently patted Anthony on the butt. "I think living with Lea has rubbed off on you."

Mary sneered. "God, I hope not!"

"It's not such a bad thing, you know…"

Mary's phone rang and she glanced at it nervously. "Greg is calling. He doesn't know I'm here, so I'm going to slip out. Just tell everyone I'm a shitty friend and leave it at that."

Brie grabbed her hand. "No, please don't go, Mary. I'll do whatever it takes to protect you."

Mary stared at Brie for a moment, then shook her head. "Price is too great."

As she got up to leave, she fished a small present from her purse and tossed it on the chair she'd been sitting on. "I'm happy for you, Brie."

Brie felt her stomach twist in a knot as she watched Mary turn and leave. Shaken by her sudden departure, Brie slowly picked up the package she'd left behind.

She opened it and found a small snow globe of the Disney castle with the words *I still believe* engraved on the stand.

Brie choked up, realizing the significance of the gift. This was not only a present to her newborn son—but a personal declaration.

Mary was reclaiming the one thing she held most dear from her childhood.

Beautiful

B rie was sleeping peacefully, curled up against Sir. She'd been up several times during the night to feed Anthony while Sir took care of Hope, who'd been too excited to sleep because of the baby.

When her phone started vibrating, Brie glanced at the name and almost ignored it. But, even in her half-awake state, the name jogged her memory and she suddenly sat straight up in the bed.

"What is it?" Sir whispered, not wanting to risk waking the baby who was sleeping in his bassinet just a few feet away.

"It's Randall Cummings, Sir."

"The lawyer involved in the film offer?"

Her heart started to race as she turned to him and nodded.

"Are you going to answer it?"

Brie stared at the phone with trepidation. "I don't want to go through that humiliation again, Sir."

"You weren't the one humiliated, my dear. The person who made the offer is the one who was turned down."

Of course, Sir was right. She held all the cards because she wasn't desperate to make the deal.

Tingles of providence suddenly coursed through Brie when she recalled a conversation she'd had with Sir during Kinky Eve, last year. At the time she had mentioned wanting to donate the money from her documentary to the Tatianna Legacy Center in Sir's honor—a million dollars to be exact.

A smile played on her lips, realizing she had the perfect opportunity to make that dream a reality.

Not only could this documentary open the minds of people all over the world, but it could also make a significant difference in the lives of the young women at Rytsar's Center.

Getting out of bed, Brie quickly tiptoed out of the room before answering it. "Hello?"

"Good morning, Mrs. Davis. I'm calling to inform you that we will be arriving at nine this morning to go over the conditions we discussed."

"So, you've agreed to let me have the final say over the film?"

"You have been granted that privilege, yes."

Brie smiled, thankful her benefactor respected her enough to grant the stipulation. Knowing that gave her the courage to lay it all on the line.

"Mr. Cummings, I have another condition."

"Mrs. Da—" he protested.

"It isn't open for negotiation. Rather than waste your time, it's best that you know it now."

He said nothing in response.

"Mr. Cummings?"

"Go on," he muttered irritably.

"The first million from my percentage will be donated to the Tatianna Legacy Center."

"The *first* million?" he scoffed.

"Yes."

"You realize you will never see a cent yourself if we agree to that."

"I don't care as long as the girls benefit from the film."

He growled. "This unnecessarily complicates things."

"Is that a no, then?" Brie pressed.

"I will postpone the meeting until I hear word back," he stated tersely. "Good day, Mrs. Davis."

Brie walked back into the bedroom and set the phone on the nightstand. When she curled up against Sir, he wrapped an arm around her, pulling her closer.

"What did Mr. Cummings have to say?" he murmured in her ear.

"I added a new stipulation." She giggled softly. "He's not happy…but is looking into it."

He nuzzled her neck before biting her lightly. "My goddess."

Brie smiled, drifting off into an easy sleep.

Brie was unprepared when Mr. Cummings called her back promptly at nine. "You have been granted your second request. Understand that further negotiation is closed."

"I understand," she replied, thrilled beyond words.

"We will be arriving within the hour."

Brie appreciated that Mr. Cummings was not ambushing her this time, the way he had during their first meeting, but such short notice was still unacceptable. "I will call my team to confirm what time they can meet."

"Time is money, Mrs. Davis," he stated irritably.

"I agree, Mr. Cummings. Therefore, both parties must respect it."

She hung up before he could reply, feeling quite pleased with herself.

After a quick call to Mr. Thompson, Brie set the meeting for eleven. Although Mr. Cummings was clearly not pleased, he agreed to the new time she set.

Brie grinned at Sir afterward. "Who would guess the day after I give birth, I would be approached with the film offer of my dreams?"

"Are you certain you are up for this, babygirl?"

"Had this happened right after Hope, I would have said no. But, for some reason, I feel stronger after this delivery." She smiled at Sir. "Of course, I'm sure that has to do with the fact that you are taking care of both children so I can rest between feedings."

He looked at her thoughtfully. "While I am incapable of sharing in the process of carrying a child, I am proficient at caring for them once they are outside the womb."

She stood on tiptoes to kiss him. "Not all fathers are as thoughtful as you."

He raised an eyebrow. "It's not just for you, my dear. I want to be a part of their lives, and part of that involves nurturing them." Sir surprised her when he started chuckling. "It seems your father has only just figured that out."

Brie smiled, remembering her plates overflowing with food. "I'm grateful old dogs can learn new tricks." She wrapped her arm around him. "But how lucky am I that you already know what kind of father you want to be?"

"Near-death experiences tend to have that effect on a person."

When Anthony began to cry, Sir started toward the bedroom to get him and asked, "Would you prefer to nurse him on the couch or the rocker?"

"I'd like to sit out on the patio, Sir."

Brie grabbed a shawl and headed outside. Although the breeze was cooler than she expected, it felt invigorating. Her spirits were incredibly high as she sat down on the patio chair and breathed in the fresh air.

She was excited that Tono was stopping by to visit. It would allow Autumn to spend extra time with Lea before they headed back across the ocean to finish their Kinbaku tour.

Brie was desperate to talk openly to Tono about his health. As much as he was fighting it, it was obvious the disease had taken a heavy toll on his body.

Sir came out carrying Anthony in one arm and Hope in the other. "She heard him wake up," he explained.

Brie took Anthony from him and smiled at her daughter. "You're taking being a big sister very seriously, aren't you, sweet pea?"

Glancing at the back door, Brie noticed Shadow sitting on his haunches, staring at them intently. "I wonder what he makes of all this."

Sir walked over and opened the door for the cat.

Shadow sauntered out and followed Sir. The big black cat settled at Sir's feet because Hope was sitting on his lap, but his eyes were locked on the new baby.

"Shadow may find it a difficult task keeping up with two little munchkins," Brie laughed.

Sir looked down at the cat. "Between the three of us, I'm certain we can keep track of these two."

Brie grinned at Shadow. "I'm definitely grateful for his devotion to Hope." Sitting back in her chair, she shook her head. "It's funny to think only two days ago, I was sitting here with a big round belly, enjoying Nonna's hot chocolate—and look at me now."

"You're even more beautiful," he said, watching her as she nursed Anthony.

She sighed with contentment. "I'm so happy right now, I wish I could stop time and live in this moment forever."

"While I appreciate the sentiment," Sir stated, glancing at Hope, "I'm far too invested in seeing what the future brings for our children."

"It is exciting, isn't it? They have their whole lives ahead of them."

His eyes flashed with pride. "We don't know what talents lay within them or what passions they will aspire to."

"And we get to be there through all of it, encouraging them every step of the way." She looked down at Anthony tenderly. "I just love being a mom!"

"It certainly suits you." Sir's tone suddenly became more serious when he said, "Whatever today brings, do not compromise what's important to you, Brie."

"I won't," she promised. "I plan to do as you've always instructed me and trust my gut."

He took her hand and kissed it. "It has never led you astray, babygirl—which I am eternally grateful for."

Brie dressed up for the meeting, making sure her hair and makeup were on point. She placed Tono's orchid in her hair, then applied bright red lipstick.

She smiled at her reflection, thinking of Ms. Clark as she carefully blotted it. The Domme's powerful demeanor was something she wanted to emulate during this meeting. Although she was a submissive by nature, when it came to her films, Brie was as fierce and protective as any Dominant.

Mr. Thompson and Mr. Phillips arrived well before eleven, giving her time to explain the new stipulation she'd added to the contract in regards to the Tatianna Legacy Center.

"That's quite admirable of you," Mr. Thompson stated.

She shook her head. "I don't see it that way. Although I have never walked in their shoes, as you know, I came close because of Lilly. If my documentary can ease these girls' suffering in any way, it would mean the world to me."

"Do you actually expect to make over a million with this film?" Mr. Phillips asked her.

Brie shrugged. "A girl can dream, can't she? Especially when it's for a good cause."

"There's no reason not to aim high, Mrs. Davis," Mr.

Thompson agreed.

"I'll need you both to verify that the contract honors the new conditions."

"Certainly," Mr. Phillips stated.

The same flock of lawyers who had attended the first meeting returned. As they entered the house, Mr. Thompson directed them to the long dining room table where Brie was waiting for them.

She made eye contact with each man as they entered. Once all of them were seated, she addressed them as a whole. "It is a pleasure to see you again."

Brie understood each person seated represented the top names in the industry, including Michael Schmidt, the greatest film editor in the business. This offer did not have only one film distributor but many, each company specializing in its own territory of the world. Mr. Cummings was quick to remind her that the documentary would not only be released in theaters, but also on DVD, cable, and digital platforms.

Truly, the offer was everything Brie ever dreamed of.

Taking the thick file from his briefcase, Mr. Cummings said, "As agreed, your percentage will go to the charity you requested up to the amount of…" He cleared his throat. "…one million dollars before the proceeds revert to you."

He slid the extensive contract over to Brie. "As we discussed, both changes have been added to the contract and are non-negotiable."

Brie looked Mr. Cummings in the eyes when she took the contract from him and then immediately placed it in Mr. Thompson's capable hands.

While she waited for her two lawyers to go through

every line Brie smiled at the gathering, feeling a sense of freedom she'd never had before. If anything was amiss, she would simply refuse to sign the contract. Brie's life would continue on the new path she'd created for herself, and she was completely at peace with that.

It was incredibly empowering!

When both lawyers finished reading through the contract, Mr. Thompson handed it back to Brie and read over the two additions with her, explaining the legalese in layman's terms.

"No other changes have been made to the original contract, Mrs. Davis. Everything is in order."

Brie felt a surge of excitement as she picked up the pen Mr. Cummings handed her. "It appears we have a deal."

She proceeded to sign her name with a dramatic flair.

The moment she set the pen down, the room erupted in applause.

"This has been a long time coming, Mrs. Davis," Mr. Cummings stated curtly, but Brie could read the relief on his face. She suddenly wondered what would have happened if he had failed to get her to sign the contract this time around.

Brie spent the next hour signing legal agreements with each company represented in the offer. Her head would have been spinning, but Mr. Phillips' knowledge of the entertainment industry proved invaluable as he explained the details of and necessity for each agreement.

By the time Brie was done signing everything, she was flying on an emotional high. "I look forward to what the future brings, gentlemen. I'm excited to see what we create together."

She stood up, and every man there immediately rose to his feet. She gave each lawyer a firm handshake as they filed out.

The last order of business was to provide Mr. Cummings with a physical copy of the documentary. It felt like a rite of passage when Brie handed it to him. "Mr. Cummings, thank you for your part in making this work."

He shook her hand firmly. "You certainly have balls for a woman."

"I'll take that as a compliment," she replied as she closed the door behind him.

When Brie turned, she saw Sir standing before her. The look of admiration on his face was something she would always remember. She ran into his arms squealing with excitement, "We did it!"

"*You* did this," he corrected as he held her tight.

"I can't believe it, Sir. It's really happening!"

"It is, babygirl. Your time has come."

Brie turned to Mr. Thompson. "Can I tell people I signed the contract if I don't discuss the terms?"

"I'm afraid not. The nondisclosure remains in effect."

She glanced at Sir. "But there's someone I need to tell. It's important."

"Your mother?"

Brie shook her head. "Mary."

"I would advise against it," Mr. Thompson cautioned her.

"Mary Wilson would never break my trust," Brie answered firmly.

She looked to Sir. His opinion was the only one that

mattered to her.

She breathed a sigh of relief when he nodded his approval.

"If it would be all right with you," she asked Sir, "I'd like to do that right now."

Sir glanced at the two lawyers.

Mr. Thompson pursed his lips, accepting the decision. "It's best we leave. We'll see ourselves out," he stated amiably, holding out his hand to Brie. "It's been a pleasure, Mrs. Davis."

Brie thanked both men profusely before grabbing her phone and heading up to her office to make the call.

To her chagrin, Mary didn't answer the first time, so she immediately called her again.

"This better be important, woman," Mary muttered, sounding distracted.

"We did it, Mary!"

"Did what?" she growled with impatience.

"I signed the contract for the film offer."

Mary was silent for a moment. "Wait…are you serious?"

"I just finished signing all the papers a few minutes ago."

"I thought the deal fell through."

"Well, the lawyer called today and agreed to everything I asked for. It's a done deal!"

"Oh, my God, Brie," Mary said breathlessly.

"I know!"

"This is the best news I could imagine."

"Mary, I couldn't have done this without you, so I wanted you to be the first to know but you can't tell anyone."

"Oh, fuck, when word gets around..." Her voice trailed off.

Brie suddenly felt the hairs stand up on the back of her neck. "Should I send Sir to pick you up?"

"No, you idiot!" she laughed. "I want to be here when Greg finds out." She suddenly lowered her voice. "Oh, my God, Brie, his whole world is about to implode. It...it..."

"What?"

"It's going to be fucking beautiful!"

Secrets

B rie couldn't wait for Tono to arrive. Unfortunately, she was not allowed to tell him the incredible news about what happened a few hours before. As soon as he walked through the door, however, Tono gave her a suspicious look.

"What's up?"

Brie blushed, then bit her lip to keep from blurting out the secret. "I'm just so thrilled to spend time with you."

Tono glanced at Sir questioningly.

"She's been rather excitable since the baby," he replied, smiling at Brie.

The Kinbaku Master looked far from convinced but accepted Brie's hug without question. She hugged him for an extra long time, instantly connecting to his spirit as he drew her in with his calming power.

When Brie broke from his embrace, she stared into his brown eyes.

Deeply concerned about his health, she insisted, "Please sit down."

"You don't have to treat me like an invalid." Tono chuckled. "I *am* capable of standing."

"How are you recovering, Nosaka?" Sir asked.

Tono looked at Sir thoughtfully for a moment before answering. "Healing from this is a slow process, not unlike what you experienced yourself."

Sir nodded. "Healing requires great patience."

Tono smiled in agreement. "Thankfully, I am a patient man."

Rather than sit on the couch with Brie and Sir, Tono joined Hope on the floor. Shadow instantly jumped into his lap and started purring.

"He's definitely missed you," Brie grinned, delighted to see the two together.

Hope scooted over to Tono. She was unusually quiet, looking up at him longingly.

"Do you want to sit on my lap, too?"

Tono gently moved the large black cat to make room for her. Hope immediately climbed into his lap and sat there smiling as she matched Tono's movements as they petted Shadow together.

"You certainly have a way with children and animals," Sir commented.

Tono grinned. "Both have a pure energy I connect with." He glanced around and asked, "Where's your son?"

"Anthony is taking a nap, but I don't expect him to be down for much longer," Brie explained.

Tono's warm smile soothed her soul. "What's it like having two?"

She smiled. "I never knew I could love two people so completely."

Tono gazed into her eyes. "Your heart has expanded."

She blushed. "It certainly feels that way. I can't wait for you and Autumn to experience it."

He nodded slowly. "We will see what the future brings."

"What are your plans after this tour?" Sir asked.

Tono sighed with a troubled look in his eyes. "I believe we should take a hiatus from traveling for my health and Autumn's wellbeing. It's time to find a place to call home."

"Here, I hope," Brie squeaked.

Tono looked down at Shadow and Hope, a smile playing on his lips. "Seeing how content Autumn is here with her friends, I think it would be a good fit."

"Oh, Tono, I'm so happy to hear that!"

Her exuberance woke Anthony up and he started fussing in the other room. Sir was about to get up when Brie stopped him. "You've been going nonstop since my first contraction. Let me take care of this."

Brie chose to stay in the bedroom while she nursed Anthony so Sir could have some time alone with Tono. She felt certain both men would benefit from the interaction.

When she finally returned to the living room, she found them talking about Faelan.

Tono looked uneasy. "After everything he's been through, I understand his struggle to hold on. It's another reason I wish to return to California."

"You have done enough for him, Nosaka," Sir assured him. "That should not play into where you choose to live. However, I understand your need to be there for him. I feel the same."

Tono looked up at Brie. "I have a favor to ask of you."

"Of course, Tono. Anything."

He reached into his pocket and pulled out a small white envelope painted with Japanese symbols. "I suspect you will see Todd before I do. Would you give this to him?"

Brie took the black and white envelope and held it tightly. "I will make sure to deliver this safely into his hands."

Tono nodded to her. "I hope it brings him some peace."

Brie went to give Sir the baby so she could put the envelope away for safekeeping, but Tono asked, "May I hold him?"

She smiled. "Your lap is already full."

"There is always room for one more."

Brie placed Anthony in Tono's arms.

He laid the baby against Shadow's back and cradled him so Hope could look at her baby brother, too. The cat did not seem to mind and continued to purr.

"An-ta-nee," Hope said solemnly.

"Your brother is named Anthony?"

She nodded, reaching out to touch his cheek. Hope squealed with laughter when Anthony grabbed her finger.

Tono looked up at Brie, his eyes twinkling. "She has your laugh."

"Does she? I never noticed."

Brie stood back to look at them. She could not describe the intense feeling of joy she felt seeing Tono on the floor with her children. It was so touching, she found herself choking up.

"Are you okay?" Sir asked quietly.

She smiled. "I'm just too happy to contain it…"

Brie felt the ache of their impending goodbye when

Lea finally arrived with Autumn to take them to the airport.

"I wish you could cancel your tour and stay with us," Brie joked.

Lea gave her a hip bump. "You guys are brimming with babies. Autumn and Tono should totally stay with me."

Autumn surprised Brie when she confessed, "After traveling for so long, I have to admit it's going to be hard to settle down. I actually like the constant travel. Every week is someplace new with a bunch of new people to meet."

Lea grabbed her arm. "Well, I'm not letting you go!"

Autumn looked at Lea longingly. "I wish you could come with us…"

"I think Hunter might have something to say about that," Lea laughed.

When Tono stood up to leave, Brie felt her heart break a little. The Kinbaku Master was like fresh air to her soul.

When she went to hug him, he whispered, "I know you are keeping something from me."

She giggled self-consciously as she pulled away.

Brie hugged Autumn next. "If you need anything, let me know."

"I've got something for you, actually." With an impish grin, Autumn told her, "Okay, fair warning, this one is a little raunchy, so forgive me. Do you know why you can never trust a baby with a dirty diaper?"

Brie shook her head in amusement.

Autumn's face turned beet red as she delivered the punch line. "Because they're full of shit."

Lea burst out laughing. "I'm adding that to my apocalypse stockpile!"

Brie giggled as she kissed Anthony's forehead. "Don't you pay them any heed, little man."

After they left, Shadow stood at the front door. Brie bent down to pet him. "I know, Shadow. It's hard, but I promise they'll be back."

Brie turned to Sir, beaming. "What an amazing day this has been."

"Truly." He wrapped both arms around her. "But now you must be a good sub and go to sleep."

"I'm not tired," she pouted.

He raised an eyebrow. "You're about to crash."

She opened her mouth to protest, but before she could, a huge yawn escaped her lips, proving he was right. Sir turned her toward the bedroom and swatted her ass. "You need to listen to your Master."

"I love you, Sir," she murmured, heading to the bedroom.

The moment Brie's head hit the pillow she was out like a light.

In the weeks that followed, time seemed to stand still as Brie grew accustomed to life with two children. She cherished this quiet moment, knowing their lives would soon be interrupted by the demands of both of their careers.

On Anthony's actual due date, Brie threw a private little party complete with balloons and party hats.

When the doorbell rang, she hurried to answer it,

expecting it to be the "due date" cake she'd ordered. Instead, she was asked to sign for a mysterious box.

"Here, let me get that for you," Sir offered when he saw the large size of it. "What did you order?" he asked, laughing as he set the box on the coffee table.

"I was just about to ask you that, Sir. So, this isn't from you?"

He shook his head.

Brie quickly opened the box to find another box inside with the name "Versace" printed on it. "I *know* I didn't order this..."

Sir took the box out and found a fancy invitation underneath. Reading it, he told her, "It appears we have been invited to attend a premiere event being held downtown."

"Who is the invitation from?"

He showed it to her. "Recognize the name?"

Brie's jaw dropped when she saw Randall Cummings signature. "Oh, my goodness. I guess the cat is about to be let out of the bag."

Sir lifted the lid of the box. "And in grand style, my dear."

Brie lifted the black dress from the box, her heart racing. The long dress had gold accents that elevated the elegance of the gown.

"Wow..." she murmured.

"The event takes place two weeks from now," he informed her.

Brie snorted, envisioning the look on Greg Holloway's face when he heard the news.

The monster was finally going to be brought down. He thought he'd won, but in reality, Holloway's demise was only two short weeks away.

Reckoning

The phone rang just minutes after the package arrived.

"Hello?"

"Mrs. Davis," Mr. Cummings answered, "I am calling to confirm you received the package."

"I certainly did."

"I trust the gown is to your liking."

She glanced at the gorgeous dress. "Very much so."

"Excellent. A limousine will pick you up the night of the event. We will be making the official announcement."

"Mr. Cummings, I know this request may sound out of left field, but I would like to bring my children."

He cleared his throat. "This is a formal event. Why would you want to do that?"

"Greg Holloway made it clear that my film would never see the light of day. He is a misogynist, and I want the world to know that a woman and mother of young children was able to defeat him."

"It would be a powerful statement, Mrs. Davis," Mr.

Cummings agreed.

"One Holloway needs to hear loud and clear."

"While I agree, we cannot have children acting as a distraction…"

Brie held her breath, expecting him to dismiss her request.

Instead, he surprised her. "…therefore, I will provide a professional nanny to assist you during the event."

Brie smiled to herself, thrilled that he was honoring the request. "Thank you, Mr. Cummings."

"It's imperative that you tell no one you received the invitation or that you will be attending."

"Why?"

"It's a strategic move, Mrs. Davis."

His answer made her even more curious about the event. "Who is going to be there?"

"The most influential people in Hollywood, including Greg Holloway."

"And he has no idea I'm coming." A slow smile spread across Brie's face.

Absolutely perfect!

"Will the person who arranged the deal be there as well?" she asked.

"I wouldn't know, Mrs. Davis."

Brie shook her head with amusement. "It does make it interesting, not knowing who is behind this. It could be any person in the room—or not."

"That would be a safe assumption."

She laughed, liking Mr. Cummings' dry sense of humor.

"I won't say a word about the event, but who can I thank for the gown?"

"I will let Donatella know it was well received."

Brie was left completely stunned. Whoever her bene-factor was, they had connections beyond her wildest dreams.

Brie slowly twirled as she gazed at her reflection in the mirror. The black V-neck gown was cinched underneath her breasts and had a long, pleated skirt that flowed gracefully when she walked. Because of the unique style of the dress, it hid her post-pregnancy belly.

An onlooker's attention would be focused on the bodice with its intricate gold highlights. This gown was elegant and classy in the way it accentuated her femininity.

Brie dressed Hope in a black dress with a yellow rib-bon around the waist. She was lucky enough to find a white onesie with a black satin vest sewn onto it for their son. Anthony looked dashing. But, even as adorable as he was, no one could compete with his father.

Sir was the picture of sophistication and class in the same black Italian suit he'd worn at their wedding. The dark vest was covered in a silvery vine pattern that matched his bow tie. He was stylish perfection all the way down to his polished Italian shoes.

"Sir, I think you're even more handsome now than you were at our wedding—and I can't believe that's even possible."

He took her hand and twirled her around as he gazed at her intently. "Brianna Renee Davis, you will dominate them tonight."

She was giddy at the thought of a submissive dominating all of Hollywood.

The limousine arrived shortly before the event was set to begin. Mr. Cummings had informed her that she would be arriving late in order to make a grand entrance. The driver arrived and knocked on their door.

When Brie answered it, he told her, "I have come to drive you and your family to the event, Mrs. Davis."

Brie glanced back at Sir and took a deep breath. "This is it…"

As they approached the vehicle, a young woman got out and formally introduced herself. "Hello, my name is Penny Warton. I'm here to assist with your children tonight."

Brie shifted Hope to her left hip to hold out her hand. "Wonderful. I'm Brie and this is my daughter, Hope."

Penny shook Brie's hand before addressing Hope. "It's lovely to meet you, Miss Hope."

The driver opened the door for Brie and bowed. "Mrs. Davis."

Brie thanked him as she helped Hope inside before sliding in herself. She could hardly believe any of this was real.

She was grateful to see that car seats for the children had been provided. When she went to buckle Hope in, Penny politely stopped her. "Please allow me, Mrs. Davis."

Brie sat back grinning as Sir slid into the vehicle and sat down beside her. Penny gently took Anthony from him and secured him into the car seat for the drive.

As the limo pulled out, Sir took Brie's hand and squeezed it in encouragement.

"After waiting so long for this moment, I can scarcely believe it's real," she confessed.

Brie couldn't wait to see the look on Mary's face when the official announcement was made. Although Mary knew the deal had been struck, she had no idea the ax was about to fall.

"Savor every moment of this night, babygirl," Sir said, kissing her lightly on the cheek.

Brie stared out the window at the tall skyscrapers as they drove into downtown LA. She thought she would be overcome with a sense of peace, but she suddenly became a bundle of nerves.

That only increased when the limousine pulled up to the Wilshire Grand and she saw the entrance teeming with reporters. Brie had never seen so many journalists gathered in one place and her heart began to race.

Memories of the hateful reception she'd received at the premiere for her first documentary flashed in her mind, and she felt a moment of panic.

"My mother is long dead," Sir reminded her, as if he could read her mind.

She nodded and closed her eyes, taking a deep breath.

My past is not my future.

The driver quickly exited the vehicle and opened the door. Sir got out first, holding Hope in one arm.

He held out his other hand to Brie. She took it, stepping gracefully out of the limousine and onto the red carpet to the sound of multiple shutters clicking. Turning back to the limousine, Brie took her son from Penny and held him tight against her to keep him from being frightened by the unusual noise and flashing lights.

"Mrs. Davis, look over here!" one of the paparazzi shouted.

The moment Sir placed his hand on the small of Brie's back, her whole body relaxed. With Sir by her side, there was nothing to fear.

Brie turned to the reporter and smiled graciously, taking Sir's advice to savor the moment rather than allow herself to be unsettled by it.

Although they were close to the entrance, it took considerable time to make it to the doors because of the many requests for their attention as the reporters clicked away.

Brie found Mr. Cummings was waiting for them inside.

She laughed in delight. "I didn't expect that kind of reception."

"This is only the beginning, Mrs. Davis," he stated, as he escorted them to the elevators.

On their way up to the top floor, Mr. Cummings explained, "You will wait until you are given the signal to enter, then your friends will follow you inside."

"My friends?" she asked, as the elevator slowed down.

He nodded as the doors opened.

Brie gasped when Sir guided her out of the elevator. The first person she spied was Master Coen.

"You're here all the way from Australia?" she cried in excitement.

The muscular Dom nodded, his eyes flashing with admiration as he looked her up and down. "I am, Mrs.

Davis."

Raven, his sub, stood beside him looking as cute as ever.

Brie shook her head in surprise when she saw that Tono and Autumn where there, too. "I can't believe you're here!"

She scanned the crowd and spotted Marquis Gray, Celestia, Lea, Hunter, Master Anderson, Shay, Boa, Mistress Lou, Ms. Clark, and Baron. Brie quickly realized that every person in the documentary was represented, except for three people—Rytsar, Faelan, and Mary.

With Sir's permission, Brie handed the baby to Penny before running to hug her friends.

"How is this even possible?" she gushed.

"Your man there made a deal we couldn't refuse," Master Coen answered, nodding to Mr. Cummings.

She looked over at him. "This is incredible. Thank you!"

Mr. Cummings only nodded in response, looking quite pleased with himself.

Brie turned to Tono and Autumn. "I never thought I would see you two again so soon."

"I've never flown in a private jet before," Autumn squealed. "It was amazing!"

"It was unexpected," Tono agreed. "But, as Master Coen stated, it was an opportunity we couldn't turn down." He looked at Brie knowingly. "And now I understand what you were hiding from me."

Brie giggled. "I signed the papers that very morning."

But it wasn't just people associated with the film who were there. Her parents, along with the Reynolds had also been invited.

"This is a proud day," Mr. Reynolds said, giving Brie a long hug. "You've fought hard for this moment."

"While raising a family, no less," Judy added, squeezing her tight.

"Brie has never been a quitter, not even when she was a little girl," her mother told them. "I couldn't be more proud of you, honey."

Brie could tell her father was uncomfortable, but he was trying hard to hide it. She understood how difficult this must be for him because of the sexual nature of her documentary. The fact he was here to support her meant more than she could say.

"I'm so happy you're here, Daddy."

"What's important to you is important to me," he replied, shifting uneasily on his feet as his eyes darted around the room. As soon as he spied the children, he gave Brie a quick peck on the cheek. "I see two grand-kids who need my attention."

Brie smiled as she watched him go. Although he was clearly out of his element, she was grateful she no longer sensed that underlying current of hostility he'd had toward her film career.

Lea came bounding up to her. "Hey, girl! This is freaking amazing."

"I can't believe it, Lea," she confessed, giving her a squeeze. "It doesn't seem real."

"I've got the most supreme joke for you…"

Mr. Cummings glanced at his watch and announced, "It's almost time."

Brie blew Lea a kiss before following Mr. Cummings down the corridor with Sir. He stopped before a large set of doors. "You will wait here. When the doors open, walk to the middle of the room and stop."

Brie took Anthony back from Penny and thanked her. Glancing back, Brie saw everyone in the film lining up behind her. She happened to catch Marquis Gray's gaze.

Her heart skipped a beat when he nodded to her with pride in his eyes.

Brie glanced at Sir holding Hope and let out a nervous breath. She was reminded of his words right after her collaring and whispered to herself, "Exude elegance and poise. Head held high but at a respectful angle."

Then the doors slowly swung open…

Brie was shocked to see Greg Holloway standing behind a podium on the stage, addressing the huge assembly.

Sir prodded her to start walking with him. Holding Anthony in her arms, Brie walked into the large room and stared at Greg with an air of confidence.

Holloway stumbled over his words when he saw her, and the room broke out in murmurs of shock. Brie walked down the middle aisle and stopped in the center of the room while Tono, Lea, Master Coen, Raven, Baron, Ms. Clark, Master Anderson, Boa, and Marquis Gray fanned out behind her.

The room suddenly grew silent.

"*What's the meaning of this?*" Holloway yelled. "Get this trash out of here." He waved his arms at the staff and pointed at Brie.

No one moved.

Holloway looked around the room for help, his face turning redder with each passing second. "Get out!" he screamed at her.

Brie shook her head slowly.

People began quietly talking amongst themselves but

still, no one moved.

Holloway pounded his fist on the podium. "Someone call the fucking police, God damn it!"

Brie looked at him with a smirk of superiority.

Her obstinance clearly infuriated Holloway, causing the man's nostrils to flare. "You don't belong here. Do you hear me? You're finished in Hollywood!"

Suddenly, a recording of Brie's voice rang out loud and clear from the speakers.

"I respectfully disagree with you on all counts."

Brie held her breath when she heard Holloway's voice next.

"I told you. This isn't up for debate, young lady."

Her jaw dropped. Brie knew exactly what this recording was. She turned to Sir and whispered, "It's the last meeting I had with Holloway…"

"My name is Brianna Davis and you will address me as such."

Holloway's recorded snarl filled the large room.

"You come in here acting as if you have skin in the game. You are nothing. *Not even a blip on the radar. So, you better learn damn quick to respect those in power and do what I say."*

"Give me good reasons to cut those scenes."

"This is not up for debate! How many times do I have to repeat myself?"

"Mr. Holloway, I'm looking for a producer who believes in this film. If you're going to rip it apart without giving me a good reason why then you're not the man for the job. It's better that we end this meeting now."

"If I don't produce this film, nobody will."

Brie's voice was cool and collected.

"Give me the disk."

The sound of the CD hitting the wall and falling to

the floor followed.

"Make the changes or that will be the fate of your precious film."

Brie remembered picking up the shattered disk and slipping it into her purse before she left.

Holloway's voice bellowed, *"If you walk out that door you will never work in this town again, Brianna Bennett."*

"My last name is Davis."

"Bennett...Davis...it doesn't matter. You don't matter!"

"You will remember my name, Mr. Holloway. One day you will see it in every theater in this nation—including here in Hollywood."

"That'll be the day," he roared, before laughing sarcastically.

"When that day comes, you'll know the truth—you have no power."

"You underestimate the influence I have in this town, little girl." His cruel laughter continued. *"You just ended your career. Better start popping out more kids. That's all you're good for now..."*

When the recording ended, the room was enveloped in a blanket of uneasy silence.

Brie smiled at Holloway, proudly holding her newborn in her arms. "I am not the one who is finished."

The top people in the industry who were involved in her new release began standing up where they sat, one after another...

Holloway stared at them all, the veins in his forehead pulsing in rage. "You're making a grave mistake, young lady."

Raising an eyebrow, Brie told him, "My name is Brianna Davis."

A large screen slowly descended on the stage as the

lights dimmed. Brie saw the shadowy figure of someone walking up to the podium to help Holloway off the stage.

Gripping music erupted as a professional trailer played on the screen, showcasing different cuts from her second documentary.

Brie stood there transfixed as snippets of the scenes flashed on the screen—Marquis with his flogger, Tono and his rope, Master Anderson with Boa, Baron and the swing, Ms. Clark with her two subs, Master Coen's playful spanking, Rytsar's sexy sadism, and Mary's scene with Faelan. The trailer ended with explosive music and the words "Coming next summer."

The excitement in the room was palpable when the lights came back up and everyone began clapping. Brie was escorted to a large table where she, Sir, and their entire entourage sat down to enjoy a world-class meal.

She looked around for Mary and found her standing with Holloway. He had a death grip on her wrist as he dragged her from table to table, talking to his old "buddies" in the film industry. It was amusing to watch them snub him in the same manner she had been snubbed at the awards ceremony.

Brie stared down at her plate, suddenly gripped with fear for Mary. She could only imagine what Holloway would do to Mary after tonight, and she seriously contemplated breaking her promise to her friend—even if it destroyed their friendship.

"Eat, my dear. You don't want to offend the host of such an extravagant party."

Brie immediately obeyed Sir, smiling as she picked up her fork. She realized her benefactor might be watching her this very moment.

As she scanned all the faces smiling back at her, Brie was startled to see Darius. He picked up his glass and held it up to her.

Brie's initial reaction was gut-level distrust because of their difficult past. However, Darius had been the only one brave enough to acknowledge her at the awards ceremony months ago. So, in recognition of that, she nodded to him.

Halfway through the extravagant meal, Mary waltzed by and turned to smile at Brie. Unfortunately, Holloway saw it and publicly berated Mary, commanding her to remember her place before pushing her back to her seat.

Marquis and Sir glanced at each other before standing in unison. The two of them walked to where Mary sat.

Holloway roared, "Stay the fuck away from her. You have no business with this one. She's mine!"

"You're wrong," Sir stated coldly. "Miss Wilson is a graduate of the Submissive Training Center. Therefore, she is under our protection."

"It's fine," Mary insisted. "I don't need any help." She shot a hostile glare at Brie, thinking she had broken her word.

"Look me in the eye and tell me you are safe with this man," Marquis commanded.

Mary glanced at Greg for a second before meeting Marquis's gaze. "I'm safe."

"You are lying to me."

Holloway jerked Mary out of her seat. "She answered your damn question. Now leave us the fuck alone!"

With lightning-fast speed, Sir broke Holloway's grip on Mary while Marquis subdued him with a pressure point.

Marquis leaned in and whispered in Holloway's ear. Brie couldn't hear his words, but whatever he said made Greg's face drain of all color.

When Marquis stepped away, Holloway stood there looking at him in stunned silence. He didn't protest, staying rooted where he stood while Sir quietly escorted Mary to the table to sit beside Lea.

"Go," Marquis commanded loudly.

The entire assembly watched in silence as Holloway slowly turned and walked out. The moment the doors closed behind him, the conversations started up again as if nothing had happened.

This night of reckoning had been beautifully orchestrated. Whoever her benefactor was, they had been artful in the execution of his demise.

After his long reign in Hollywood, Greg Holloway had been effectively erased.

Sir patted Marquis's back before sitting back down beside Brie. "I'd say this is turning out to be an eventful night on many fronts."

He picked up his champagne glass and held it up to Brie.

She looked at her friends and family gathered at the table. Mary wouldn't even look at her, but Brie didn't mind because Mary was safe, and that was all that mattered.

Clinking glasses with Sir, Brie replied, "I couldn't agree more, Sir."

The rest of the evening was a whirlwind as the greatest talents in Hollywood, who would soon be working with her, waited patiently for their chance to speak with Brie.

She felt like the belle of the ball.

Remind Me

B y the time they returned home, Brie was flying on such an emotional high that she was uncertain if she would ever be able to fall asleep.

When Penny mentioned that she had been hired to care for the children for the entire evening and would be happy to put the children to bed while they celebrated privately, Brie smiled. "That was incredibly thoughtful of Mr. Cummings."

"I agree," Sir replied, "and we shall take advantage of your offer."

Once inside, Sir handed Anthony to Brie, motioning her to the couch, "Wait here, Mrs. Davis."

While Brie nursed Anthony, Sir asked Penny to join him while he put a tuckered out little Hope to bed. Once the baby was fed, Penny took him and retired upstairs to look over the children—leaving them alone together.

Sir held out his hand to Brie. "Now that Hollywood knows who you are, let me remind you who you are to me…"

Brie took his hand and he led her into the bedroom.

Sir called out the code and the door to their playroom slowly opened.

"Although this dress is stunning, it does not compare with what lies underneath," he murmured as he unzipped the designer gown. It pooled around her feet, and he helped her step out of it.

Sir caressed her shoulders lightly before undoing her bra and letting it fall to the floor. He then knelt to help her out of her shoes. Sir caressed the arch of her foot, stating, "I appreciate the sensual lines of heels, but I much prefer your feet bare, babygirl."

He stood and picked Brie up in one swift motion, carrying her to the binding table. Laying her down on it, Sir abruptly left.

Brie bit her lip, wondering what he had planned. He returned a short time later with a bowl of warm, soapy water and a cloth. He began by removing the heavy makeup she had applied for the special event.

After leaving to refresh the water, Sir tenderly bathed the rest of her body in silence. By the time he was finished, Brie felt completely refreshed and new.

Sir left again. On his return, he'd stripped off his jacket and shirt, allowing Brie to admire his masculine chest.

"Kneel before your Master," he commanded.

She purred in pleasure as he helped her off the table. She felt tingles of excitement as she lowered herself to the floor.

"There is nothing more intoxicating than a powerful woman giving her submission to me."

"It is my deepest honor," she said breathlessly as she bowed her head low at his feet.

"Tonight, we will revisit a significant moment between us."

"If it pleases you," she responded excitedly.

"You should know that I am breaking protocol here," Sir began. "I have wanted to take your sweet little ass ever since I saw you bend over the box of cigarettes at the tobacco shop."

His words sent shivers through Brie. He was role-playing that second night of training when he'd met her after class...

"I understand, Sir."

"You can refuse me."

She quivered in anticipation. "I do not wish to, Sir."

"Very well."

He commanded her to mount the table on all fours. Helping her onto it, he buckled the leather cuffs, strapping down her wrists so she was resting her weight on her forearms. He then buckled her ankles in place, leaving her with her legs spread and her ass in the air.

Being bound to the table the same way she had been that first time aroused Brie in ways she could not explain, and she gushed with wetness.

Standing back, Sir leaned against the wall and stared at her. Brie basked in his intense gaze. All those feelings from their first night together bubbled up inside of her.

"Some men think they need toys to excite a woman, but I do not believe that. I firmly believe in the power of touch."

Brie had never forgotten those powerful words and stared at him longingly.

Sir didn't move as he continued to gaze at her.

Brie knew it was another tool in his arsenal and

smiled to herself. Sir was keenly aware that making her wait only made her want him that much more.

She held her breath when Sir finally pushed away from the wall and walked toward her. She felt butterflies the moment his hand lightly brushed the curve of her back.

Every fiber of her being was focused on her Master's touch.

Sir smiled leisurely as his fingers explored her. The electrical current caused by his touch ignited her desire, making her nipples hard and her pussy wet. He reached one hand between her legs and felt her wet panties.

"It appears your body is aching for me to fuck that sweet little ass."

Brie nodded, whimpering as he pushed the material of her panties aside to penetrate her pussy with his middle finger.

"Desperate for me, are you?" he asked, pulling his finger out and teasing her swollen clit.

Moving behind her, Sir pulled her panties down to her knees. "Ah, yes," he murmured appreciatively, his hand grazing her buttocks. "Such a fine ass."

Sir pressed his thumb against her throbbing clit and rubbed it slowly, fanning the fire. When his hand was drenched with her excitement, he slipped his finger into her ass.

Brie moaned softly, loving his invasion.

"My little sub wants my cock stroking her in the ass," he stated confidently.

She nodded eagerly without any shame.

"Beg for it."

"Please, Sir. Fuck my ass with your cock," she

time. The intensity of her climax consumed her—just before she felt the warm gush of her watery come.

"Yes," Sir murmured huskily.

Brie let out mewing noises afterward, totally spent by their sensual power exchange. Sir pulled out slowly, weak from the encounter.

She looked back at him and smiled, noticing the look of vulnerability in his eyes. It was the same look she'd seen that first night.

"I love you," she said fervently, grateful for this scene of remembrance.

Sir met her gaze and smiled. "I never told you, because I refused to admit it to myself at the time, but that night I knew I would never let you go."

Late in the night, after Penny left and Brie had checked on both children, she curled up against Sir's naked body.

Brie lay there in pure bliss, thinking back on all the people she'd spoken to that evening. Their enthusiasm for her documentary left no doubt that this unprecedented collaboration was going to be something truly extraordinary.

"Best night ever," she murmured dreamily.

"Exceptional," Sir agreed, pulling her closer to him.

But, as perfect as the evening was, Brie knew things were not over with Greg Holloway. The man was used to getting his way, and he was especially cruel in his revenge whenever he didn't. Brie knew he would be gunning for her after the spectacular way he had been dethroned in front of all his peers.

It gave Brie great comfort to know Mary had the protection of the Submissive Training Center behind her now. The trainers at the Center were a wall of protection that Holloway could not breach.

But something else needled at Brie's heart, and she struggled to fall asleep despite her exhaustion. "Sir?"

"Yes, babygirl."

"I missed having Rytsar and Faelan there tonight."

"Their absence was unfortunate but understandable."

She snuggled against him. "Still, I feel…" She searched for the right word. "…unsettled by it."

"If I'm honest, I felt troubled by it, as well."

Time passed slowly as she lay in the dark, fighting to sleep.

Wondering if Sir had succumbed, she whispered, "Are you still awake?"

"I am," he answered in a serious tone. "However, I know what will help us both fall asleep faster."

She turned in his arms to face him. "What?"

"We will make a stop in Russia before we visit Nonno and Nonna."

An acute sense of relief flooded through Brie. "That would ease my heart."

"Go to sleep now," he commanded gently, kissing her forehead. "I need you to be well-rested for what lies ahead."

I hope you enjoyed *The Ties That Bind!*

Reviews mean the world to me.

TWO BOOKS COMING UP NEXT – The Cowboy's Secret & the Next Brie Book #23!

Preorder Now

The Cowboy's Secret
Standalone novel in the Unleashed Series
(Coming September 2021)

Master Anderson, the Bullwhip Master, is determined to leave his mark in the world—and in the bedroom.

The sexy cowboy with a heart of gold has a secret that will move you.

His story has all the feels.

AND

A Heart Unchained:
Brie's Submission Book 23
(Coming December 2021)

A trip to Russia will rock Brie's world, and an extended visit to Italy warms her heart when Nonna holds their second child for the first time.

In solidarity, the community bands together to help one

of their own as a new father fights to hold on.

But Brie is about to stumble on a tragic secret involving Sir's family.

Can the passionate connection between a Dom and his beloved submissive heal a shattered heart?

COMING NEXT

The Cowboy's Secret
Standalone in The Unleashed Series
Available for Preorder

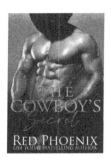

A Heart Unchained
Book 23 of the Brie's Submission Series
Available for Preorder

Reviews mean the world to me!

I truly appreciate you taking the time to review
The Ties That Bind.

If you could leave a review on both Goodreads and the
site where you purchased this eBook from, I would be so
grateful. Sincerely, ~Red

ABOUT THE AUTHOR

Over Two Million readers have enjoyed Red's stories

Red Phoenix – USA Today Bestselling Author
Winner of 8 Readers' Choice Awards

Hey Everyone!

I'm Red Phoenix, an author who also happens to be a submissive in real life. I wrote the Brie's Submission series because I wanted people everywhere to know just how much fun BDSM can be.

There is a huge cast of characters who are part of Brie's journey. The further you read into the story the more you learn about each one. I hope you grow to love Brie and the gang as much as I do.

They've become like family.

When I'm not writing, you can find me online with readers.

I heart my fans! ~Red

To find out more visit my Website

redphoenixauthor.com

Follow Me on BookBub

bookbub.com/authors/red-phoenix

Newsletter: Sign up

redphoenixauthor.com/newsletter-signup

Facebook: AuthorRedPhoenix

Twitter: @redphoenix69

Instagram: RedPhoenixAuthor

I invite you to join my reader Group!

facebook.com/groups/539875076052037

SIGN UP FOR MY NEWSLETTER
HERE FOR THE LATEST RED
PHOENIX UPDATES

FOLLOW ME ON INSTAGRAM
INSTAGRAM.COM/REDPHOENIXAUTHOR

SALES, GIVEAWAYS, NEW
RELEASES, PREORDER LINKS,
AND MORE!
SIGN UP HERE
REDPHOENIXAUTHOR.COM/NEWSLETTER-
SIGNUP

Red Phoenix is the author of:

Brie's Submission Series:

*You can also purchase the AUDIO BOOK **Versions**

Also part of the Submissive Training Center world:

Rise of the Dominates Trilogy
Sir's Rise #1
Master's Fate #2
The Russian Reborn #3

Captain's Duet
Safe Haven #1
Destined to Dominate #2

Unleashed Series
The Russian Unleashed #1
The Cowboy's Secret #2

Other Books by Red Phoenix

Blissfully Undone
* Available in eBook and paperback

(Snowy Fun—Two people find themselves snowbound in a cabin where hidden love can flourish, taking one couple on a sensual journey into ménage à trois)

His Scottish Pet: Dom of the Ages
* Available in eBook and paperback

Audio Book: *His Scottish Pet: Dom of the Ages*

(Scottish Dom—A sexy Dom escapes to Scotland in the late 1400s. He encounters a waif who has the potential to free him from his tragic curse)

The Only One
* Available in eBook and paperback

(Sexual Adventures—Fate has other plans but he's not letting her go…she is the only one!)

Passion is for Lovers
* Available in eBook and paperback

(Super sexy novelettes—*In 9 Days, 9 Days and Counting, And Then He Saved Me*, and *Play With Me at Noon*)

Varick: The Reckoning
* Available in eBook and paperback

(Savory Vampire—A dark, sexy vampire story. The hero navigates the dangerous world he has been thrust into with lusty passion and a pure heart)

eBooks

Keeper of the Wolf Clan (Keeper of Wolves, #1)

(Sexual Secrets—A virginal werewolf must act as the clan's mysterious Keeper)

The Keeper Finds Her Mate (Keeper of Wolves, #2)

(Second Chances—A young she-wolf must choose between old ties or new beginnings)

The Keeper Unites the Alphas (Keeper of Wolves, #3)

(Serious Consequences—The young she-wolf is captured by the rival clan)

Boxed Set: Keeper of Wolves Series (Books 1-3)

(Surprising Secrets—A secret so shocking it will rock Layla's world. The young she-wolf is put in a position of being able to save her werewolf clan or becoming the reason for its destruction)

Socrates Inspires Cherry to Blossom

(Satisfying Surrender—A mature and curvaceous woman becomes fascinated by an online Dom who has much to teach her)

By the Light of the Scottish Moon

(Saving Love—Two lost souls, the Moon, a werewolf, and a death wish…)

Play With Me at Noon

(Seeking Fulfillment—A desperate wife lives out her fantasies by taking five different men in five days)

Connect with Red on Substance B

Substance B is a platform for independent authors to directly connect with their readers. Please visit Red's Substance B page where you can:

- Sign up for Red's newsletter
- Send a message to Red
- See all platforms where Red's books are sold

Visit Substance B today to learn more about your favorite independent authors.

Made in the USA
Coppell, TX
21 September 2023

21857803R00134